Extraordinary P:
Swimming in th.

"*Swimming in the Dark* is captivating both for its shimmering surfaces and its terrifying depths. I began reading, and soon realized I wouldn't be doing anything else that day. I needed to see these boys, these lovers, through to the end. Tomasz Jedrowski is a remarkable writer, alive to the ramifications of history and politics, in which the violence of a corrupt state can never fully stamp out the flourishing of beauty, grace, and resistance."
—Justin Torres, bestselling author of *We the Animals*

"Summer can be a time to wander in a forest until you get lost, skinny-dip in a lake by moonlight, fall in love. . . . Experience some of those moments through [*Swimming in the Dark*]."
—NPR, *All Things Considered*

"An affecting and unusual romance, with a political undercurrent. . . . Jedrowski writes elegantly and evokes the emotional honesty that the lovers first thrive in, and then the grimly repressive machinery of the [Polish United Workers' Party]."
—*The Guardian* (UK)

"This debut novel by Tomasz Jedrowski shows how easily love can be torn apart."
—*Harper's Bazaar* (UK)

"A beautiful novel, and at its heart an amazing love story."
—BBC Radio 4, *Open Book* (editor's pick)

"Dazzling. . . . Readers will relish the indelible prose, which approaches the mastery of Alan Hollinghurst. Jedrowski's portrayal of Poland's tumultuous political transformation over several decades makes this a provocative, eye-opening exploration of the costs of defying as well as complying with social and political conventions."
—*Publishers Weekly* (starred review)

SWIMMING

IN THE

DARK

A Novel

TOMASZ JEDROWSKI

WM

WILLIAM MORROW

An Imprint of HarperCollinsPublishers

P.S.™ is a trademark of HarperCollins Publishers.

HarperCollins books may be purchased for educational, business, or sales promotional use. For information, please email the Special Markets Department at SPsales@harpercollins.com.

Originally published as *Swimming in the Dark* in the United Kingdom in 2020 by Bloomsbury.

A hardcover edition of this book was published in 2020 by William Morrow, an imprint of HarperCollins Publishers.

FIRST WILLIAM MORROW PAPERBACK EDITION PUBLISHED 2021.

Designed by Leah Carlson-Stanisic

Library of Congress Cataloging-in-Publication Data has been applied for.

ISBN 978-0-06-289001-6

24 25 26 27 28 LBC 13 12 11 10 9

To Laurent, my home.

As to the action which is about to begin, it takes place in Poland—that is to say, nowhere.

—Alfred Jarry
Ubu Roi

Wszystko mija, nawet najdłuższa żmija.
(Everything passes, even the longest of vipers.)

—Stanisław Jerzy Lec
Unkempt Thoughts

SWIMMING
IN THE
DARK

I DON'T KNOW WHAT WOKE me up tonight. Not the branch of the chestnut tree knocking against my window, not *Pani* Kolecka coughing in the room next door. Not anymore. Maybe it was the ghosts of these noises, swept up by the wind, carried across the ocean to knock on my consciousness. Maybe. What I am certain of is this: my body feels depleted, like a foreign country after a war. And yet I cannot go back to sleep.

I think of you. The face that my memory can conjure up with its rough outlines and fine details, with the gray-blue eyes the same color as the Baltic Sea in winter. I think of your face while I get up, while I move in the darkness from bed to window, clothes lying around the floor like unfinished thoughts. And then I recall yesterday evening, and the chill of it makes me stop in my tracks. The radio was on, song hour like every day after work: something light was playing, I can't remember what. I was standing in the kitchen looking for the coffee when the music stopped.

"We are interrupting the program for a special announcement," said the lady in her soft, round voice. *"This morning, on December the thirteenth, martial law has been declared in the Socialist Republic of*

Poland. It follows weeks of strikes and unrest by pro-democracy pro-testers and the meteoric rise of the first independent trade union of the communist bloc, Solidarność" (mispronounced). *"In a televised ad-dress, the government announced a series of drastic measures: schools and universities have been shut down, the country's borders have been closed, and curfews have been imposed on the population. We will keep you updated on any further developments."*

The music went on.

I can't even tell you what I felt in that moment. It was the pur-est form of paralysis. My body must have shut down before my mind could react. I have no idea how I made it into bed.

I light a cigarette by the window. Outside, the street is empty, and the night's rain shimmers on the pavement, reflecting the two-story buildings and crackling neon. "24 hours," says the hamburger joint down the block. "Wanda's Greenpoint Conve-nience," whispers another in red and white. Police sirens wail in the distance. Bizarrely, they are the same as at home. Whenever I hear one, the hair on my forearms stands on end. They remind me of the night when that same shrill sound filled the air of a city far away. Before that city became an outline, an item on the foreign news. Before loneliness covered me like night-blue tar.

I don't know whether I ever want you to read this, but I know that I need to write it. Because you've been on my mind for too long. Ever since that day, twelve months ago, when I got on a plane and flew through the thick layers of cloud across the ocean. A year since I saw you, a year that has felt like limbo—

ever since then, I've been lying to myself. And now that I am stuck here, in the dreadful safety of America, while our country is falling apart, I am done with pretending that I've erased you from my mind. Some things cannot be erased through silence. Some people have that power over you, whether you like it or not. I begin to see that now. Some people, some events, make you lose your head. They're like guillotines, cutting your life in two, the dead and the alive, the before and the after.

It's best to start with the beginning—or at least what feels like it. I realize now that we never much talked about our pasts. Maybe it would have changed something if we had; maybe we would have understood each other better and everything would have been different. Who can say? Either way, I probably never told you about Beniek. He came more than a decade before you. I was nine, and so was he.

CHAPTER 1

I HAD KNOWN HIM ALMOST all my life, Beniek. He lived around the corner from us, in our neighborhood in Wrocław, composed of rounded streets and three-story apartment buildings that from the air formed a giant eagle, the symbol of our nation. There were hedges and wide courtyards with a little garden for each flat, and cool, damp cellars and dusty attics. It hadn't even been twenty years since any of our families had come to live there. Our postboxes still said *"Briefe"* in German. Everyone—the people who'd lived here before and the people who replaced them—had been forced to leave their homes. From one day to the next, the continent's borders had shifted, redrawn like the chalk lines of the hopscotch we played on the pavement. At the end of the war, the east of Germany became Poland and the east of Poland became the Soviet Union. Granny's family was forced to leave their land near Lwów. The Soviets took their house and hauled them on the same cattle trains that had brought the Jews to the camps a year or two earlier. They ended up in Wrocław, a city inhabited by the Germans for hundreds of years, in a flat only just deserted by some family we'd never know, their dishes still in the sink, their bread crumbs on the table. This is where I grew up.

It was on the wide pavements, lined with trees and benches,

where all the children of the neighborhood played together. We would play catch and skip ropes with the girls, and run around the courtyards, screaming, jumping onto the double bars that looked like rugby posts and on which the women would hang and beat their carpets. We'd get told off by adults and run away. We were dusty children. We'd race through the streets in summer in our shorts and knee-high socks and suspenders, and in flimsy wool coats when the ground was covered in leaves in autumn, and we'd continue running after frost invaded the ground and the air scratched our lungs and our breath turned to clouds before our eyes. In spring, on Śmigus-Dyngus Day, we'd throw bucketloads of water over any girl who wasn't quick enough to escape, and then we'd chase and soak one another, returning home drenched to the bone. On Sundays, we'd throw pebbles at the milk bottles standing on the windowsills higher up where no one could steal them, and we'd run away in genuine fear when a bottle broke and the milk ran slowly down the building, white streams trickling like tears down the sooty facade.

Beniek was part of that band of kids, part of the bolder ones. I don't think we ever talked back then, but I was aware of him. He was taller than most of us, and somehow darker, with long eyelashes and a rebellious stare. And he was kind. Once, when we were running from an adult after some mischief now long forgotten, I stumbled and fell onto the sharp gravel. The others overtook me, dust gathering, and I tried to stand. My knee was bleeding.

"You all right?"

Beniek was standing over me with his hand outstretched. I reached for it and felt the strength of his body raise me to my feet.

"Thank you," I murmured, and he smiled encouragingly before running off. I followed him as fast as I could, happy, forgetting the pain in my knee.

Later, Beniek went off to a different school, and I stopped seeing him. But we met again for our First Communion.

The community's church was a short walk from our street, beyond the little park where we never played because of the drunkards, and beyond the graveyard where Mother would be buried years later. We'd go every Sunday, to church. Granny said there were families that only went for the holidays, or never, and I was jealous of the children who didn't have to go as often as me.

When the lessons for the First Communion started, we'd all meet twice a week in the crypt. The classes were run by Father Klaszewski, a priest who was small and old but quick, and whose blue eyes had almost lost their color. He was patient, most of the time, resting his hands on his black robe while he spoke, one holding the other, and taking us in with his small, washed-out eyes. But sometimes, at some minor stupidity, like when we chatted or made faces at one another, he would explode, and grab one of us by the ear, seemingly at random, his warm thumb and index finger tight around the lobe, tearing, until we saw black and stars. This rarely happened for the worst behavior. It was like an arbitrary weapon, scarier for its randomness and unpredictability, like the wrath of some unreasonable god.

This is where I saw Beniek again. I was surprised that he was there, because I had never seen him at church. He had changed. The skinny child I remembered was turning into a man—or so I thought—and even though we were only nine, you could already see manhood budding within him: a strong neck with a place made out for his Adam's apple; long, strong legs that would stick out of his shorts as we sat in a circle in the priest's room; muscles visible beneath the skin; fine hair appearing above his knees. He still had the same unruly hair, curly and black; and the same eyes, dark and softly mischievous. I think we both recognized the other, though we didn't acknowledge it. But after the first couple of meetings we started to talk. I don't remember what about. How does one bond with another child, as a child? Maybe it's simply through common interests. Or maybe it's something that lies deeper, for which everything you say and do is an unwitting code. But the point is, we did get on. Naturally. And after Bible study, which was on Tuesday and Thursday afternoons, we'd take the tram all the way to the city center, riding past the zoo and its neon lion perched on top of the entrance gate, past the domed Centennial Hall the Germans had built to mark the anniversary of something no one cared to remember. We rode across the iron bridges over the calm, brown Oder River. There were many empty lots along the way, the city like a mouth with missing teeth. Some blocks had only one lonely, sooty building standing there all by itself, like a dirty island in a black sea.

We didn't tell anyone about our escapes—our parents would not have allowed it. Mother would have worried: about the red-faced veterans who sold trinkets in the market square with their cut-off limbs exposed, about "perverts," the word falling from her lips like a two-limbed snake, dangerous and exciting. So we'd sneak away without a word and imagine we were pirates riding through the city on our own. I felt both free and protected in his company. We'd go to the kiosks and run our fingers over the large, smooth pages of the expensive magazines, pointing out things we could hardly comprehend—Asian monks, African tribesmen, cliff divers from Mexico—and marveling at the sheer immensity of the world and the colors that glowed just underneath the black and white of the pages.

We started meeting on other days too, after school. Mostly we went to my flat. We'd play cards on the floor of my tiny room, the width of a radiator, while Mother was out working, and Granny came to bring us milk and bread sprinkled with sugar. We went to his place only once. The staircase of the building was the same as ours, damp and dark, but somehow it seemed colder and dirtier. Inside, the flat was different—there were more books, and no crosses anywhere. We sat in Beniek's room, the same size as mine, and listened to records that he'd been sent by relatives from abroad. It was there that I heard the Beatles for the first time, singing "Help!" and "I Want to Hold Your Hand," instantly hurling me into a world I loved. His father sat on the couch in the living room reading a book, his white shirt the brightest thing I'd ever seen. He was quiet and soft-spoken, and I envied Beniek. I envied him because I had never had a real father, because mine had left when I was still a child and hadn't cared to see me much since. His mother I remember only vaguely. She made us grilled fish, and we sat together at the table in the kitchen, the fish salty and dry, its bones pinching the insides of my cheeks. She had black hair too, and although her eyes were the same as Beniek's, they looked strangely absent when she smiled. Even then, I found it odd that I, a child, should feel pity for an adult.

One evening, when my mother came home from work, I asked her if Beniek could come and live with us. I wanted him to be like my brother, to be around me always. My mother took off her long coat and hung it on the hook by the door. I could tell from her face that she wasn't in a good mood.

"You know, Beniek is different from us," she said with a sneer. "He couldn't really be part of the family."

"What do you mean?" I asked, puzzled. Granny appeared by the kitchen door, holding a rag.

"Drop it, Gosia. Beniek is a good boy, and he is going to Communion. Now come, both of you, the food is getting cold."

One Saturday afternoon, Beniek and I were playing catch on the strip outside our building with some other children from the neighborhood. I remember it was a warm and humid day, with the sun only peeking through the clouds. We played and ran, driven by the rising heat in the air, feeling protected under the roof of the chestnut trees. We were so caught up in our game that we hardly noticed the sky growing dark and the rain beginning to fall. The pavement turned black with moisture, and we enjoyed the wetness after a scorching day, our hair glued to our faces like seaweed. I remember Beniek vividly like this, running, aware of nothing but the game, joyous, utterly free. When we were exhausted and the rain had soaked through our clothes, we hurried back to my apartment. Granny was at the window, calling us home, exclaiming that we'd catch a cold. Inside, she led us to the bathroom and made us strip off all our clothes and dry ourselves. I was aware of wanting to see Beniek naked, surprised by the swiftness of this wish, and my heart leapt when he undressed. His body was solid and full of mysteries, white and flat and strong, like a man's (or so I thought). His nipples were larger and darker than mine; his penis was bigger, longer. But most confusingly, it was naked at the tip, like the acorns we played with in autumn. I had never really seen anyone else's, and wondered whether there was something wrong with mine, whether this is what Mother had meant when she'd said Beniek was different. Either way, this difference excited me. After we had rubbed ourselves dry, Granny wrapped us in large blankets, and it felt like we had returned from a journey to a wondrous land. "Come to the kitchen!" she called with atypical joy. We sat at the table and had hot black tea and waffles. I cannot remember anything ever tasting so good. I was intoxicated, something tingling inside me like soft pain.

Our Communion excursion arrived. We went up north, toward Sopot. It was the sort of early summer that erases any memory of other seasons, one where light and warmth clasp and feed you to the absolute. We drove by bus, forty children or so, to a cordoned-off leisure center near a forest, beyond which lay the sea. I shared a room with Beniek and two other boys, sleeping on bunk beds, me on top of him. We went on walks and sang and prayed. We played Bible games, organized by Father Klaszewski. We visited an old wooden chapel in the forest, hidden between groves of pine trees, and prayed with rosaries like an army of obedient angels.

In the afternoons we were free. Beniek and I and some other boys would go to the beach and swim in the cold and turbulent Baltic. Afterward, he and I would dry off and leave the others. We'd climb the dunes of the beach and wade through its lunar landscape until we found a perfect crest: high and hidden like the crater of a dormant volcano. There we'd curl up like tired storks after a sea crossing and fall asleep with the kind summer wind on our backs.

On the last night of our stay, the supervisors organized a dance for us, a celebration of our upcoming ceremony. The center's canteen was turned into a sort of disco. There was sugary fruit *kompot* and salt sticks and music played from a radio. At first we were all shy, feeling pushed into adulthood. Boys stood on one side of the room in shorts and knee-high socks, and girls on the other with their skirts and white blouses. After one boy was asked to dance with his sister, we all started to move onto the dance floor, some in couples, others in groups, swaying and jumping, excited by the drink and the music and the realization that all this was really for us.

Beniek and I were dancing in a loose group with the boys from our room when, without warning, the lights went off. Night had already fallen outside, and then it rushed into the room. The girls shrieked, and the music continued. I felt elated, suddenly high on the possibilities of the dark, and some unknown barrier receded in my mind. I could see Beniek's outline near me, and the need to kiss him crept out of the night like a wolf. It was the first time I had consciously wanted to pull anyone toward me. The desire reached me like a distinct message from deep within, a place I had never sensed before but recognized immediately. I moved toward him in a trance. His body showed no resistance when I pulled it against mine and embraced him, feeling the hardness of his bones, my face against his, and the warmth of his breath. This is when the lights turned back on. We looked at each other with eyes full of fright, aware of the people standing around us, looking at us. We pulled apart. And though we continued to dance, I no longer heard the music. I was transported into a vision of my life that made me so dizzy my head began to spin. Shame, heavy and alive, had materialized, built from buried fears and desires.

That evening, I lay in the dark in my bed, above Beniek, and tried to examine this shame. It was like a newly grown organ, monstrous and pulsating and suddenly part of me. It didn't cross my mind that Beniek might be thinking the same. I would have found it impossible to believe that anyone else could be in my position. Over and over I replayed that moment in my head, watched myself pull him into me, my head turning on the pillow, wishing it away. It was almost dawn when sleep finally relieved me.

The next morning we stripped the sheets off our beds and packed our things. The boys were excited, talking about the disco, about the prettiest girls, about home and real food.

"I can't wait for a four-egg omelet," said one pudgy boy.

Someone else made a face at him. "You voracious hedgehog!"

Everyone laughed, including Beniek, his mouth wide open, all his teeth showing. I could see right in to his tonsils, dangling at the back of his throat, moving with the rhythm of his laughter. And despite the sweeping wave of communal cheer, I couldn't join in. It was as if there were a wall separating me from the other boys, one I hadn't seen before but which was now clear and irreversible. Beniek tried to catch my eye, and I turned away in shame. When we arrived in Wrocław and our parents picked us up, I felt like I was returning as a different, putrid person and could never go back to who I had been before.

We had no more Bible class the following week, and Mother and Granny finished sewing my white gown for the ceremony. Soon, they started cooking and preparing for our relatives to visit. There was excitement in the house, and I shared none of it. Beniek was a reminder that I had unleashed something terrible into the world, something precious and dangerous. Yet I still wanted to see him. I couldn't bring myself to go to his house, but I listened for a knock on the door, hoping he would come. He didn't. Instead, the day of the Communion arrived. I hardly slept the night before, knowing that I would see him again. In the morning, I got up and washed my face with cold water. It was a sunny day in that one week of summer when fluffy white balls of seeds fly through the streets and cover the pavements, and the morning light is brilliant, almost blinding. I pulled on the white high-collared robe, which reached all the way to my ankles. It was hard to move in. I had to hold myself evenly and seriously, like a monk. We got to the church early, and I stood on the steps overlooking the street. Families hurried past me, girls in their white lace robes and with flower wreaths on their heads. Father Klaszewski was there, in a long robe with red sleeves and gold threads, talking to excited parents. Everyone was there, except for Beniek. I stood and looked for him in the crowd. The church bells started to ring, announcing the beginning of the ceremony, and my stomach felt hollow.

"Come in, dear," said Granny, taking me by the shoulder. "It's about to begin."

"But Beniek—"

"He must be inside," she said, her voice grave. I knew she was lying. She dragged me by the hand, and I let her.

The church was cool, and the organ started playing as Granny led me to Halina, a stolid girl with lacy gloves and thick braids, and we moved down the aisle hand in hand, a procession of couples, little boys and little girls in pairs, dressed all in white. Father Klaszewski stood at the front and spoke of our souls, our innocence, and the beginning of a journey with God. The thick, heavy incense made my head turn. From the corner of my eye I saw the benches filled with families and spotted

Granny and her sisters and Mother, looking at me with tense pride. Halina's hand was hot and sweaty in mine, like a little animal. And still, no Beniek. Father Klaszewski opened the tabernacle and took out a silver bowl filled with wafers. The music became like thunder, the organ loud and plaintive, and one by one boy and girl stepped up to him to get on their knees as he placed the wafer into our mouths, onto our tongues, and one by one we walked off and out of the church. The queue ahead of me diminished and diminished, and soon it was my turn. I knelt on the red carpet. His old fingers set the flake onto my tongue, dry meeting wet. I stood and walked out into the blinding sunlight, confused and afraid, swallowing the bitter mixture in my mouth.

The next day I went to Beniek's house and knocked on his door with a trembling hand, my palms sweating beyond my control. A moment later I heard steps on the other side; then the door opened, revealing a woman I had never seen before.

"What?" she said roughly. She was large, and her face was like gray creased paper. A cigarette dangled from her mouth.

I was taken aback and asked, my voice aware of its own futility, whether Beniek was there. She took the cigarette out of her mouth.

"Can't you see the name on the door?" She tapped on the little square by the doorbell. "KOWALSKI," it said in capital letters. "Those Jews don't live here anymore. Understood?" It sounded as if she were telling off a dog. "Now don't ever bother us again, or else my husband will give you a beating you won't forget." She shut the door in my face.

I stood there, dumbfounded. Then I ran up and down the stairs, looking for the Eisenszteins on the neighboring doors, ringing the other bells, wondering whether I was in the wrong building.

"They left," whispered a voice through a half-opened door. It was a lady I knew from church.

"Where to?" I asked, my despair suspended for an instant.

She looked around the landing as if to see whether someone was listening. "Israel." The word was a whisper and meant nothing to me, though its ominous rolled sound was still unsettling.

"When are they coming back?"

Her hands were wrapped around the door, and she shook her head slowly. "You better find someone else to play with, little one." She nodded and closed the door.

I stood in the silent stairwell and felt terror travel from my navel, tying my throat, pinching my eyes. Tears started to slide down my cheeks like melted butter. For a long time I felt nothing but their heat.

Did you ever have someone like that, someone that you loved in vain when you were younger? Did you ever feel something like my shame? I always assumed that you must have, that you can't possibly have gone through life as carelessly as you made out. But now I begin to think that not everyone suffers in the same way; that not everyone, in fact, suffers. Not from the same things, at any rate. And in a way this is what made us possible, you and me.

CHAPTER 2

WE WERE ON THAT bus together. Warszawa, 1980. It was warm, the beginning of June, the summer after our final university exams. And although we'd been in the same year throughout our studies, we didn't know each other. You'd never gone to lectures, never needed to. So we could have just as well never met.

The bus was waiting for more people to arrive. I sat by the window, the orange wool curtains drawn to block out the sun, rereading *Quo Vadis*. I cared less about the religious part than about the love story, the heroic turns, the bravery of opposition. This is how I lived back then—through books. I locked myself into their stories, dreamt of their characters at night, pretended to be them. They were my armor against the hard edges of reality. I carried them with me wherever I went, like a talisman in my pocket, thinking of them as almost more real than the people around me, who spoke and lived in denial, destined, I thought, to never do anything worth recounting.

I drew back the curtain and looked at myself in the reflection of the window. There were days that I liked what I saw—the long, arched nose, the almond-shaped eyes. But most days not. Most days I felt a dull reproach against myself, an alienation from my twenty-two-year-old body.

The bus was filling up, the atmosphere giddy, laced with the promise of summer. The seat next to me was empty until Karolina appeared and hurled herself onto it, her big-mouthed smile tinged with her particular kind of sarcasm.

"Ready to be turned into a peasant?" she said.

I put the book on my lap. "Can't wait," I said, trying to look deadpan.

Karolina laughed, throwing back her head. "And I can't wait to see you getting down and dirty in those fields."

The bus was almost full now, and the driver climbed in, cigarette glued to his lips, and off we went. We vibrated with the rhythm of the clattering engine. Sun streamed onto my face, and outside, the spire of the city's symbol—Stalin's Palace of Culture—reached so high into the soft-blue sky it made your neck hurt to look at it. I was strangely elated. I had always liked the act of leaving, the expanse between departure and arrival when you're seemingly nowhere, defined by another kind of time. This journey reminded me of the ride I'd taken four years earlier: the day I'd taken the train to Warszawa for the first time by myself, to come to the capital, to leave my old self behind. I'd stood on the platform with Granny, two large suitcases next to us, a handkerchief in her gloved hand dabbing her glassy eyes. She didn't want me to go, but she didn't say anything. I was eighteen, itching to leave. I'd kissed her hastily and gotten on the train, feeling selfish to be leaving her, dragging the suitcases to my compartment, passing smoking soldiers leaning out of the window in the narrow corridor. I'd settled into my compartment, between men in worn suits and women in hats, drinking tea from flasks and peeling apples and eating boiled eggs wrapped in white-lace cloths like christened babies. The train had moved off, and I'd fallen into a lull, villages sunk in forests rushing past. Selfish. Growing into yourself is nothing but that.

Our bus drove onto a bridge to cross the Wisła. The trees were a clear green, and the banks of the river filled with them like a head of dense curls. The smell of linden trees and lilac was in the air, sweet and colorful and intoxicating, submerging the city. The sandy shores were deserted, making the whole embankment appear wild. If it hadn't been for the tops of the gray tower blocks just behind the thickness of the trees, it would have looked as if no human had ever lived here.

I turned back to Karolina. She was smoking, her wide lips painted coral red and leaving a mark on the mouth of the cigarette. I can't remember ever having seen her without that lipstick or without the dark-blond fringe that framed her unruly eyes.

"You're all right?" she asked, cocking her head. I nodded and couldn't help but smile. I was glad to have her with me. We'd met in first year, and since then she'd become like a sister to me. It was she who'd taught me half of what I cared to know. She had a stack of under-the-counter books, which we read and discussed together. She'd introduced me to Simone de Beauvoir and Miłosz, to the poems of Szymborska and the travel accounts of Kapuściński. Sometimes, she'd compare our country with Haile Selassie's Ethiopia and declare we needed a similar revolution. I admired her courage to speak her mind.

"*Please*," she'd say, and pull her eyebrows together whenever I'd ask if she wasn't afraid of speaking out. Mother and Granny had fed me stories of terror, of people they knew back in the day disappearing for one critical comment.

"Stalin's been dead for a long time," Karolina would say. "We know the system is a farce; *they* know it's a farce. And we're not in East Germany, thank God. Here they're sleepwalking."

The countryside began, and we bumped along the roads past vast fields and birch forests and endless stretches of pines and little tired towns with church spires sticking out. I don't know whether Karolina fully knew about me—I think she suspected it. But she never pushed me, never confronted me, and I have always been grateful to her for that. It's the sort of subtlety I'm not sure I would have had in her place. Only once did she come close to overstepping the line. It was a month or so before the camp, after a play at the National Theatre—we'd gone to see Mrożek's *Tango*. We felt like a drink, and she took me to a small bar tucked away in a narrow side street in the Old Town. She said that was where the actors went. The place was full of smoke and dark animated figures by the bar, spilling out onto the pavement. It felt like the beginning of summer. I could tell what many of those men were but, at first, didn't want it to be real. There was an exuberance about them that disturbed me deeply. It was their curling voices, the "darlings" that padded their sentences, their quick, voracious eyes, the movement of their hips as Donna Summer moaned "I Feel Love" over hypnotic electric beats, a song I had loved and now berated myself for ever having liked. They threw one furtive glance at me and I felt see-through. Karolina didn't seem to notice anything unusual—there were women too, relaxed and sly and loud. I looked at her sideways, wondering whether she was really oblivious or just pretending. I wanted to leave right then and there, wanted to stop noticing, stop searching for a face that I would desire and could never have, but Karolina ordered us drinks and I managed to stay and talk and to keep my eyes mostly on her. By the time our beers were almost empty, I'd grown restless and angry, asked her why she had brought me there. She was casual, as always. She said a friend had recommended the place.

"What friend?" I asked.

She made a face like she was thinking. "You wouldn't know him."

I nodded, smiled ironically. "Fine. Can we leave now?"

Her face was unchanged, as if she hadn't heard me. She drank the rest of her beer in one go, put her money on the bar, and got up from her stool. "Let me just go to the bathroom."

She walked off, and I stood alone in the crowd, feeling entirely powerless, an embarrassed child in the midst of pleasures he couldn't grasp. No, it was worse than that. Beside me, two old men in suits who had appraised us spoke in excited voices.

"You know, darling," said one to his friend, in a stage whisper, with a fur collar around the lapel of his jacket, sounding drunk, "you must read that unpublished Baldwin I told you about. It moved me to tears. If that won't make you wake up, nothing will."

The other one—very thin—nodded. "You'll pass it to me, will you, darling?"

"Yes, but be careful with it, you know it's not even my copy, it's hers"—and he pointed at a man in a white silk shirt across the bar, deep in conversation with what looked like one of the actors from the play we had seen, a pretty boy with wavy blond hair and a small, upturned nose.

After this, Karolina came back from the ladies' and we left. I was determined to take nothing from that place, not one memory, not one conclusion for myself. But like stones thrown into the sky with all one's might, pieces of that night—the boys and the men who wanted them, the flirtation, the codes of seduction

I could only guess at—returned to me with even greater intensity than I had lived them. The law of gravity applies to memories too. And one day, as I sat in the library trying to work, to clear my mind, I remembered the book. I found his name in a catalogue of the foreign literature department. Baldwin. James. There was a list of his works, and only one of them had no official translation: *Giovanni's Room*. This had to be it, I thought. I shut the catalogue, tried to forget about it. But the title wouldn't leave me in peace, tantalizing like a loose tooth. I set out for it. And after weeks of searching, weeks of questions to suspicious-looking shop attendants who'd tell me there was no such book, that it had never been translated, I got lucky. It was just a few days before camp, in a tiny *antykwariat* bookshop that specialized in art and history, run by a man who could have been a friend of those men in the bar. He shot me a meaningful, almost amused look, then walked off to a back room and returned with a rustling brown-paper package.

When it was time to pack for the camp, I tore off the cover and glued the pages neatly into another book, burying it deep down at the bottom of my bag.

Our bus arrived at the end of the afternoon, as the sun was getting weaker but hadn't yet begun to set. The camp lay just outside a village, surrounded by low wooden fences and lined by a little river on one side. The bus stopped in front of the main building, a wide concrete bungalow with a clock on its facade and a set of flags (white and red, hammer and sickle) hanging limply from its front. A short, stout man in a uniform watched us with small, attentive eyes as we climbed out of the bus, slightly dizzy, shaken from the ride.

"I'm Comrade Leader Belka," he boomed, commanding us

to line up in front of him. There was something imperious in his voice and something both weary and angry about his manner. It was the same anger and weariness I'd observed in my schoolteachers, those who struggled to believe in the system yet punished others for doing the same. "Welcome to the work education camp," Belka called out, walking up and down the line we'd formed. "I congratulate you for having signed on for this important service." Our faces were impassive, but the irony of his words couldn't have escaped anyone. The camp was obligatory—no one would be allowed to graduate without participating. He continued his speech, extolling the importance of agricultural work, the role of the working classes in our socialist struggle, and the duty, even for "intellectuals" (he grimaced at the word), to contribute to the efforts of the fatherland. Obedience was key, he said.

It was the same spiel we'd heard all our lives, with more or less conviction. I turned my head and looked along the line to find Karolina, but instead my eyes fell on you. I had never seen you before—not consciously, anyway. Yet my mind felt strangely relieved, as if it had recognized someone. You were as tall as me, broad-shouldered, and your eyes were light, contrasting with your dark hair. You were looking at Belka, concentrating, and I took a moment to take you in, unguarded, forgetting myself. As if by instinct, like an animal suddenly aware of being watched, you turned your head toward me, and before I could avert my gaze, our eyes met, locked for an infinite, interminable instant in mid-air. A flash of heat traveled from my stomach to my cheeks, my thoughts jumbled like a ball of string. I turned my head as quickly as I could. For the rest of the speech I looked straight at the comrade leader, my mind scrambling for composure, stumbling over itself.

When Belka had finished, we grabbed our bags from the bus and were assigned to the different wooden huts scattered around the campgrounds. I was in one with three other guys, Wojtek, Darek, and Filip. They were nice boys, strangely immature and innocent. We shared two bunk beds, a table, and two chairs. We went to have dinner in the canteen, served by an army of women in aprons and deflated paper bonnets, standing behind the counter as if someone had left them there many years earlier. A large lady with an immobile face served the tomato soup with rice, while an ageless-looking girl with reddish skin piled on beetroot mash and potatoes. I sat with Karolina and the boys from my hut. They spoke easily, joking and jesting. But I wasn't really there. I looked around the canteen, across the long tables and through the tangled voices and ringing cutlery, until I spotted you: sitting at a table at the other end of the room, deep in conversation with a girl, your head turned toward her. In the stark white light of the canteen your black hair glistened, and there was something strangely focused about you, something light yet unyielding in your eyes that stirred both envy and desire in me. It was as if your presence already overpowered me, like a prophecy I was unable to read.

That night I lay awake in bed, the other guys fast asleep around me, the moon pouring in through the half-open curtain. Sharp memories knocked on the door of my consciousness, and what came to me was an old nightmare, one I had often dreamt as a child, one that had descended upon me with cruel frequency before and after Beniek's departure.

In it I stood in an endless overgrown field. Everything was still, as if petrified, and an overbearing silence reigned. There was no one—not just near me or within earshot, but anywhere. With the inexplicable logic of dreams, I was certain that I was alone in this world, the last member of a forsaken race. I looked around and started to see rectangular stones reaching out of the grass. They were blank and smooth, and I knew they were tombstones. They were watching me. Their stillness made my heart race with panic; standing there was like an infinite fall. It all seemed so undeniably real, not like a dream but a premonition. I'd feel violated upon waking. Outside, in the darkness of the night, the branch of a chestnut tree would sway in the wind and scratch against my window like a monster demanding admission, and without thinking I'd get out of bed and tiptoe across the cool wooden floor to my mother's room. We would sleep together, her enveloping me from behind with her arms around my tummy, her stale, warm breath above my head, us breathing in unison, small and large, breathing in and out until the morning when the darkness would be gone and Granny would come to stir us, scolding us as we rubbed clusters of sleep from the corners of our eyes.

"It isn't right—you two, so close," she once said, waking us. "What's to become of a man if he sleeps in the same bed as his lonely mother?" Her voice took on a raspy tone that came directly from her spiky throat.

"Mama, he had a bad dream. And he's not a man. He's still only a child," said my mother, hoisting herself up, taking her hands off me. My grandmother's face remained bitter.

"He's growing up, Małgosia, even if you think he's still a boy. And without a man in the house to show him the ropes, in this house of *babas,* who knows what kind of a soft man he will become?"

"Could you please not make everything about men?" cried my mother.

"I'm not soft!" I shouted, standing up in bed. "And Mama doesn't need another man. I can take care of her."

"And when you go away and marry someone else?" Granny asked, her voice becoming shrill and mean, as if imitating my own. "What will Mummy do then, huh? Will she be all alone?"

"I will never get married," I said. "Never. I won't ever leave Mama."

"See what I mean?" said Granny, looking at my mother. "See what you're turning the boy into? *Abnormal*."

"I'm not abnormal!" I screamed, collapsing on the bed and clenching my fists around my mother's duvet. Shame throbbed behind those words, a snake brushing past, underneath a blanket of leaves. Late some nights, when the growing unwanted desire stopped me from sleeping, I would yield to its current. I would let the hidden fantasies sweep me away, listen to their murmur, of the boys and their bodies, the hard forms of their whiteness, the smell of sweat and musk and skin. Moments from PE would flicker: thighs in shorts and armpits in sleeveless tops; Henryk, the strongest boy in the class, on the leather-wrapped gymnastic rings, hanging above us all in the gymnasium, his biceps flexing, the dark hair of his armpits contrasting with his skin, precocious veins running all along his arms, the bulge in his short white shorts . . . images from the changing rooms, the showers we took afterward—water trickling down backs, along the cross of chests and into belly buttons, down to the strongholds of their cocks, which I would only dare glimpse at for a moment and imprint onto my mind despite myself.

When I was done and my body had given its release, I would

push these thoughts away, deep down into the recesses of my mind. And yet I'd wake with the same images stuck in my head, like flies caught on a strip of glue. Years of yearning compressed like a muscle, pulsating mercilessly. I felt like a gas flame left burning on the stove for no reason.

One day after school, right before my final exams, when I could no longer take it, I didn't go straight home but walked through the city by myself, feeling the world far away from me. I walked without knowing where I was going, taking in the shreds of conversations of couples dressed for their dates in suits and ties and skirts and blouses, with their hair done, the man carrying the woman's coat and making a joke, looking her over in approval; past groups of girls coming out of school in their uniforms, long blue skirts and white socks drawn to their knees, walking in pairs with their plaited hair dangling behind them like tails; past groups of silent smoking men with red faces sitting on benches drinking from unlabeled bottles. The city was dirty and broken, layers of soot and age on the facades, nothing clean and nothing clear, a murky secondhand world. It felt like I would never get away, not from myself, not from this. I walked and walked, and my legs and feet hurt, and this was the only thing that stilled me a little.

On the other side of the river the sun was setting on the cathedral's broken towers. Shops began to close, and men and women in black shoes hurried out of buildings and started queuing for buses. I wasn't going home. I stood near the old market hall, seeing the women leave with their net bags filled with vegetables and loaves of bread, and I walked in, saw the vendors pack up their goods. Upstairs I wandered along the iron walkways and past the little shops, just underneath the massive swooped roof with its lamps and iron elevators. In one shop an old man stood behind the counter, his thin white hair combed neatly across his scalp. There was only one light bulb in the place, hanging from the ceiling not far from his face, and something made me enter. Bottles without labels stood on shelves behind him. "One liter," I said. He looked me over with vague curiosity and grabbed a bottle from behind him. I paid him with my pocket money.

The bottle was hidden in my coat as I walked toward Staromiejski Park, the one near the river. It was the park where everyone knew the "inverts" went. I found a bench right outside it and watched the mothers and couples clear out as night fell, taking sips from the bottle that burned my mouth and throat, burned right through the inside of me. Pain followed by relief.

When I felt sufficiently powerful and clouded, I entered the dark mouth of the park. It seemed empty at first. Still, I started to tremble with fear and possibility.

There was a bench facing away from the river, lit by the faint moon. I sat down and felt my body shaking and my knees jumping all by themselves. I took some more sips and looked around, my eyes adjusting to the dark. A figure appeared on the path. He approached slowly and sat beside me. I was scared to look into his face. He asked me how old I was, his voice gentle and dry.

"Eighteen," I lied, and sensed him nod.

"You're a good-looking boy. What are you doing out here at night?" I knew I was still trembling. He put his hand on my knee, calming my body. "You're nervous, no?" he said.

I nodded, reassured by the contact, finally daring to look at him. It struck me straight away how old he was—he could have been my father—and how worn his face, as if life had already claimed the best parts of him, leaving only a husk. And yet, his hand on me felt good. He took out a flask from the inside pocket of his jacket and handed it to me. I took a sip, sensing his smell on the bottle top, and, without wanting to, imagined him undressed above me. The power of that possibility intoxicated me along with the spirit burning my throat.

"Come on," he said, taking the flask from me and letting his hand travel along my thigh, "let's go. We'll be better somewhere more quiet." He stood without waiting for my reaction, and I followed him. I followed him into complete darkness, toward a hole in the bushes so black it felt like I was blind. My steps were uncertain. At some point he stopped, me bumping into him, the two of us suddenly facing each other. The darkness was a comfort: it was as if we'd melted into the night and nothing that would happen would be fully real. He began to stroke my neck, his fingers rough and callused, and his sharp breath on my face. My heart was threatening to break out of my chest. With a hurried but practiced hand he loosened the belt of my trousers and pulled out my cock, which welcomed the touch of unknown fingers and summer air. He knelt down, disappearing from my vision, and enveloped me in the warm cave of his mouth. It was the best feeling. It felt like I was gliding down a tunnel, or that it was riding through me. My head thrown back, I saw the stars in the sky. Then I heard his fly unzipping and sensed him masturbating, rapid, urgent movements that excited me. And as we rode like this, him panting and me gasping, the urgency and abjection rose within me like heat, like an irrepressible scream, mounting, pushing, taking over, until the lights went off and I closed my eyes and exploded in his mouth, warmth and wetness meeting in one great, terrible relief.

I wanted to run home straightaway, knew I had to get away

from that place, and remembered Granny, who'd already be worried to death. But I didn't. Because after I had released myself in this stranger's mouth, it almost felt like I no longer had a home. So, after he had finished with a low grunt and we'd zipped up, we returned to the bench, where we had met on the other side of my life, and began to talk, our barriers suddenly removed. He unwrapped story after story, and I kept asking him questions, feeling it was my duty to learn. He told me about his first time, in the forest with a farmer from his village. He told me how he'd been in the war and how he'd almost died, and how he'd been raped by Russian soldiers in a prison camp. I nodded and said I was sorry and made myself feel nothing. I couldn't allow his pain to penetrate me.

"Do you live with your family?" I asked quickly.

He laughed. He lived on his own, he said, in a single room in one of those large bourgeois apartments the Germans had built when the city was still called Breslau, the same apartments that were now ruins and which housed up to a dozen people. He shared his kitchen and bathroom with three families, each one in a single room. He came to the park every night, he said. I don't know why he was so honest with me, but it made me feel less alone.

"What about finding someone you could . . ." I hesitated. "Love."

He huffed, and smiled for the first time, revealing a set of gray teeth. "As a *ciota*, a fag," he finally said, "you will always be lonely. And you will learn to bear it. Some have a wife and children"—he nodded his head—"like that one you saw walking past earlier, but they are the worst. They can stand themselves even less. At least I'm free." He looked across the dark park, lit a cigarette, and exhaled the smoke into the night. "We give and take love for one night, maybe a couple of weeks. But not longer than that. There is too much resentment. Too much hatred. You live for pleasure if you're like this, and hope the police won't stop you. Mind you, they've stopped me a couple of times, but I've always managed to talk my way out."

His words haunted me for a long time afterward. I had told him my name—he had told me his, and I felt as if I owed it to him—but I never wanted to relapse, to come near the sordid temptation again. I never wanted to be like him. My greatest terror was ending up alone. Yet part of me was sure that's how I would end up, and that it was the worst thing that could happen to someone. I knew I would not be able to bear it. I decided never to go back to the park, never to look at the boys in class the same way again, to reform myself. After that night, when I went home, and Granny ran toward me and asked me where I had been and cried and smelled alcohol on my breath and slapped me and hugged me, I decided I would not let the bad in me take over.

It was around that time, or shortly after, that I met Jolka. She was a friend of a friend from school, and I knew she liked me. I'd watched her compete in the school gymnastics championships, and her body—firm and tall and slim—was unlike those of the other girls, whose softness and roundness scared me. One night, at a school dance in the gymnasium, I kissed her little mouth to the sound of Maryla Rodowicz, the song's melancholy filling the room as I tried to get lost in something I knew would never cover me entirely. Just above our heads hung the gymnastic rings, giving off their scent of leather and sweat.

That week I took Jolka by the hand and walked her up and down our street. Granny and Mother watched us from the kitchen window. They were beaming with pride.

————

On the first morning of camp they woke us early, storming into the hut and blowing a whistle, leaving us just enough time to brush our teeth in the washrooms and have some milk soup and tea in the canteen. In the coming weeks, I realized the canteen always smelled of cabbage and grease no matter what we were having, as if the entire building had been soaked in a concoction of the two shortly before our arrival. Every day we'd queue for something we didn't really want, which gradually became the only thing we knew.

After breakfast we were given our uniforms, a pair of green shorts and a green shirt, the same for boys and girls. They were made of stiff, rough cotton that felt like canvas on my skin. The morning sun was cool on our thighs and arms as we left the hut to assemble once again in front of the main building. The comrade leader's eyes hovered over us with petty satisfaction.

"For the coming weeks you'll be picking beetroots from the fields over there," he barked, pointing beyond the camp's fence. He called out names from a list and divided us into teams.

When my name was called, I joined a group standing to one side. I didn't recognize anyone except for you. My stomach made an involuntary jump. We went around introducing ourselves, and when it came to you, you shook my hand—yours padded and large and warm—and said your name in that low, clear voice that spoke of natural confidence. I could hardly respond. Your face was broad and solid, well-constructed, with high cheekbones like outposts guarding your eyes, narrow and intensely gray-blue.

"Pleased to meet you," you said. "I'm Janusz."

Janusz. Two syllables that rise and fall and follow each other logically, almost inevitably, and whose sound together is so familiar, so natural, that the meaning of its parts remained hidden to me until years later: *Ja,* meaning "I" in our language, and *nusz,* sounding just like our word for "knife."

The comrade leader's whistle screeched in the air as he gestured us across the camp. I let myself fall behind as the groups started to move, pained and relieved to see you walking ahead. We reassembled on the huge field that seemed to have no end and watched as the comrade leader and a farmer from the village, a man with a red face, wearing woolen trousers and an old shirt, rolled up at the sleeves, showed us how to pick the beets: breaking up the earth around them with our hands, grabbing the point where the leaves meet the bulb, pulling hard to tear out the plant with its roots. Each group was given a portion of the field to work, along with baskets and gloves. We had from nine until five each evening to reach our quotas.

"And don't procrastinate, comrades!" Belka cried, trying to look at all of us at once. "I will be patrolling the fields."

The whole operation seemed foreign to me, and as we started working, my body felt like a metal construction, heavy and unyielding. I had to kneel in the brown earth to get a grip on the beets, and my mind was agitated. You were in the first row, as if leading us, moving nimbly with your legs bent and your back straight. The workings of your leg muscles showed just underneath the skin, tendons contracting like strings being drawn, veins running down your lower arms and confounding themselves like rivers on a map. Your hands were strong and bulky, with square nails and fingers thick like screwdriver handles. *Those aren't city hands,* I remember thinking.

After a while, my body started to ache, but seeing you like that made me push ahead too. The sun grew stronger, throwing its warmth on to our arms and legs and the backs of our heads. As we moved along, sweat started to form—discrete drops at first, here and there, on the forehead and on the tips of our spines, and then, as we continued, little streams trickled, fueled by our movement. I pushed on, feeling the pain in my body, but beyond that, sensing that it had started to give way. I was surprised by the energy that lay beyond the discomfort. The rhythm made me move on, the touch of the earth and the feel of the plants becoming hypnotic. The smell was humid and pungent and fresh. It made me think of Aunt Marysia's garden outside Wrocław, with its berry bushes and fruit trees and places where one could hide, and beyond its fence nothing but fields. I hadn't thought of that in ages. Mother would take me there when I was a child, and I'd play for hours by myself, dig and find worms and beetles and hold the soil, have it crumble in between my fingers, try to eat it.

I worked with the earth, forgot myself in it. Farther out, there were other groups, all bent over the beets, breathing with effort, the sky open and wide. We broke for lunch, and afterward we napped in our huts for an hour before going back to work, the sun milder then, our bodies cooler. When we had worked for longer than enough, the comrade leader's whistle sounded across the field to mark the end of the day. I hurt in places I had never been aware of before and went to bed exhausted, sleeping more deeply than I had since childhood.

I got used to the sight of you, but we never spoke. In the breaks, the group would rest in the shade of a hut by the edge of the field, and you and some other boys smoked, and I chatted with the girls. But not with you. I avoided you, so that you couldn't avoid me. I didn't want to be in the field of your power. I envied your lightness and the beauty you carried with such ease.

At mealtimes I sat with Karolina and Beata, a friend from lectures. She was short and round-faced and busty, quick to laugh and quick to be frightened. She told us she was getting married right after the camp was over, to a guy from the year below.

"You're not pregnant, are you?" asked Karolina, looking concerned.

"God, no!" cried Beata, blushing a little.

"Because you know you cannot trust condoms," Karolina said, pretending not to notice Beata's deepening color. "Some of those old hags in the shops pierce them with the tiniest of needles and sell them on like that. They can't bear to see us having fun. So really, you need the pill. If you want to, I'll take you to my doctor. She's a woman, and she won't ask if you're married."

Beata had turned beetroot-red and shook her head. "We've only been going out for six months," she muttered, looking at her plate. "But the Bureau will give flats to married couples as a priority. I'm sick of living with my parents."

"Darling, that can take forever," said Karolina, trying not to sound mean. "Two years or more. But maybe you'll be lucky."

While the two of them talked, I watched you on the other side of the hall, sitting with the same girl I'd seen you with the night before. She wore a denim jacket, new and brilliantly blue, something that one could only buy with dollars at the government Pewex stores. I stared at her, transfixed. She wasn't exactly pretty—not at first sight, with her straight dark hair parted so plainly in the middle. But there was something very cool and self-assured about her, in the way she held her body and smiled at you while you spoke. Next to her sat Maksio Karowski, a bulky guy who was notorious for being the son of a high Party official and for trying to seduce almost every girl (and mostly succeeding).

On some nights, after work, Karolina and Beata and I would walk to the village nearest to the camp. We'd sit on a bench in the square, underneath some fruit trees, facing a wooden church, and we'd watch old couples stroll past, women with flowered kerchiefs covering their hair and men with canes and hats and faces as worn as their shoes. We'd go to the only shop in the village to see whether they had cigarettes or soda (mostly they didn't). Beata would whisper that this was a sign of the economy collapsing soon, and Karolina would laugh.

"The economy has been collapsing ever since we were born," she said one evening, her painted lips parting, revealing her large teeth. "Our beloved Party Chairman Gierek has borrowed so much money from the West that even our grandkids won't be able to pay our debts. But before anything *actually* happens, I'm the one who's going to collapse—from countryside-induced boredom." She lit a city cigarette, took a deep toke, and let the smoke escape through her nostrils.

The church bell started to ring, and a flock of swallows chased invisible insects in the fading light. I began to think of what I would do with myself after the summer. Years earlier, the children I'd played with outside our flat had gone to work in factories, in shops, on buses, or in the mines, while I'd gone to the capital to study. Work had seemed like the beginning of the end, university a prolonging of youth. I'd enjoyed it, despite its limitations—we couldn't read what we wanted and were meant to see the decadence of capitalism in all Western texts, even if most professors barely pretended to care about the Party. But now that my studies were over, I had no idea what would come next. One of my literature professors had taken a liking to me and mentioned something about a possible doctorate. But I suspected he'd try to make me study something foolish, something politically useful, a topic I'd be stuck with for years. And I knew I wouldn't be able to stand teaching. Not with a lifetime of lousy pay, not with the simple truths everyone knew, our longing for Western comforts, our hatred for the Soviets, unmentionable or punished with dismissal.

In those days I had no idea where I was going, and the work at the camp seemed to offer little release. The sun was merciless, and my body revolted against the effort, refusing to sweat. As I broke up the earth and pulled on the beets, my thoughts would snap back to you, to the bar where Karolina had taken me, to the void stretching out before me. I fought against them (the thoughts and the beets), fought their stubbornness, their toughness. I fought them, and they fought me, until I tore them out and the next one came. By now I was faster, stronger. I no longer had to kneel in the earth. I stood up like you, bent at the knees and back straight. But it was still a struggle; the real fight was not with the earth or the plants. Slowly, slowly, I found a rhythm. I stopped fighting. I stopped thinking. One day, as I worked away like this, sweat began to release itself. I allowed the union between the earth and my body, I let go, and for the first time in my life I appreciated everything for what it was, observed the miracle of it. The earth for being the earth, my hands for being my hands, the plants for growing out of seeds, and the others around me, everyone, with their own rights and dreams and interior worlds. Sweat poured over me more than ever, drenched my face, swept across the thick of my brows into my eyes, flooded down my neck and down my back like a deluge, and I accepted its gift. It was as if the sweat had washed away the past and all the thoughts and fears of the future and all that remained was now, clean and light and ever-dancing.

That evening I left the others behind and went for a walk. The evening was mild. I crossed the fence, went past the beetroot fields, until I reached a small river. Red and yellow poppies grew by its bank, and tall grasses moved in the breeze. The murmur of the water calmed me, weaving itself into my subconscious. I kept walking. On the other bank, a hare ran across a field, stopping at the sight of me, ears propped up like furry ferns, tiny nose flickering up and down. There we stood, the two of us, motionless, taking each other in. Finally, he turned his head and hopped off.

It did me good, that walk. It reminded me of the aimless ones I would take in Wrocław, when I could no longer stand being in the same space as Granny or at school. There was nowhere I could be without being with others, having to interact or to act. Even on my walks around the block, neighbors greeted and appraised. There were times when I'd get on the tram and ride across the city. I would get off at the last stop, in a neighborhood where no one knew me, and I'd wander, not

thinking, looking at the unknown streets and houses and people and feeling free and anonymous. Like an unwritten piece of
paper. I'd forgotten the pleasure of this, and then and there, by
the river, with the fields stretching out before me and the camp
far behind me, something of that freedom returned. The water
was clear, and at the bottom I could see the bed of pebbles and
light-brown mud and small fish swimming to and fro.

I continued on, not thinking about where I was going until
I stopped, not quite knowing why. There was something large
moving in the water. Someone was swimming. The back of a
head—black wet hair glued to it—moved away from me, and I
stood and watched, seeing without being seen. Broad shoulders
and fine back muscles moved in a quick, confident crawl, head
underwater, coming up for air every couple of strokes. Before
I knew it, the figure had turned around and started to swim in
my direction. It got closer and closer with each move. The sun
was behind me, and I threw a long shadow onto the water. As
soon as the figure swam through this dark stretch, it stopped
and raised its head.

You wiped your eyes with the back of your hand and stood
up in the water, which was only waist-deep.

"Hello," you said, sounding like you didn't know who I was.
Streams of water trickled down your torso. Your body was slim
and strong, your chest and stomach drawn with lines and divi-
sions, their own rules of gravity.

"Hello," I said, torn between wanting to run and watching you.

You squinted and held your palm flat over your brow against
the sun behind me. "You're from our group, no?"

I nodded.

"I'm Janusz," you said with an easy smile. You seemed almost offensively comfortable standing there. I was the one feeling naked.

"I'll let you get on. Didn't mean to disturb." I turned to leave.

"And you?"

I turned back around. "Me what?"

You laughed. It was a light and joyous sound, self-sufficient and contagious. "You have your head in the clouds, no? Your *name*."

I laughed too, feeling myself blush.

"I'm Ludwik. Ludwik Głowacki." It struck me how little my name meant to me, how absurd it was in its attempt to contain me.

You nodded. "Nice to meet you properly. Don't you want to try the water?" Your arms moved around in it. "It's perfect."

"Thanks. I don't really swim."

You looked at me funny. "You don't know how to swim?"

I shook my head. "No, that's not it. I just don't like to do it."

"Not even in this heat? Why not?" You laughed, incredulous, your smile mocking and charming.

I shrugged and walked a couple of steps backward. "Maybe another day."

"OK," you said, nodding. "Another day. I'm here almost every evening."

"See you, then," I said, walking off. After a few steps I turned around, despite myself. Your body was gliding through the water, leaving a trail of ripples on its surface.

The next day I saw you more clearly than I had before, as if you'd been drawn against the background of the others. I let myself look at you, watched you at work and when you spoke to the people at your table, especially the black-haired girl with her Western clothes. There was an inherent elegance to your way of being, an ease with yourself and the world, as if no fear had ever penetrated your mind, as if the path you walked on was pliable and ready to be molded by your feet. And yet we didn't speak and didn't acknowledge each other, except for a small nod and a small knowing smile you gave me on the field. Other than that, our meeting had been off-site, off the record.

That evening I went to the same spot by the river, but you weren't there. And so I lay in the grass and looked at the sky and listened to the water. I wondered whether you hadn't come in order to avoid me, or what else it could mean. Then I sensed movement, a presence nearby, and I got up. There, across the high grass, a body lay on the ground, almost hidden. I approached silently. You were lying spread out on your back, one hand beneath your head, the other on your stomach. Eyes closed. The hand on your stomach rose and fell in the slow and steady rhythm of your breath, T-shirt slightly lifted, revealing your tanned midriff and the path of fine hair leading down. I stood frozen for a moment, looking at you, afraid you'd wake up and see me like this. Your long eyelashes. The beautiful veins on your arms. All I wanted was to stand there and take you in. You opened your eyes, gray-blue and brilliant. You looked at me, and my heart skipped a beat.

"Hey." Your voice sleepy.

"Hey. Did I wake you?" I took a few steps back, feeling out of place.

You heaved yourself up onto your elbows, closed your eyes with force, and opened them again. "I think so. Which is a good thing. I'd have slept until tomorrow morning." You ran your hands over your face, yawning, and then turned to me as if registering me properly for the first time. "So you came." You smiled. "You came to learn how to swim after all?"

"I told you I know how to swim."

You stood and stripped off your T-shirt, running past me and jumping into the water in your trunks.

"Then prove it!" you called, emerging from the water, your hair wet and dark.

"Nah. Not that easy."

"C'mon! Just your feet, then. You'll see how good it is." You waved me over.

I went to the water's edge, where you were standing expectantly, and looked at the surface. It was see-through, with green, scintillating weeds swaying in the current like wheat in the wind. Your eyes said "C'mon," and I stepped in. Soft, smooth mud gave way to the soles of my feet, coolness enveloped my ankles.

"See what you've been missing out on?" you said, and looked at me with a smile. Late-afternoon light danced on the water and reflected on your face like a caress. I couldn't say anything, only managed to nod. My belly was knotted and light. You wanted me to get in completely, but I said no. My refusal made you laugh and me even more uncomfortable. "Before camp is over, you'll be swimming here without any hesitation," you said, diving in and leaving me standing there in my clothes, the water reaching up to my knees.

I got out and sat by the bank, watching you swim. The sky was turning a darker blue. I wasn't sure what I was doing there, but I knew I didn't want to leave. Finally, you emerged, water trickling down your body, hair sticking to your head, striking me with the reality of your presence.

"So why do you come here by yourself, anyway?" I asked as you were drying off. I tried not to stare. "Why are you not with your friends?"

You laughed your light laugh. "What friends?"

I shrugged, trying not to blush. "I always see you sitting with the same people in the canteen."

"Oh yeah?" Your smile became teasing. Then, to my relief and dismay, you pulled on your T-shirt. "I don't know," you said, your head appearing through the neck of the T-shirt. "Why are *you* not with your friends?"

"I guess it's nice to be away from the crowd sometimes, to be able to hear yourself think. I go mad when I'm surrounded by others all the time."

"I guess it's the same for me, then," you said, turning around and pulling off your swim shorts, revealing your behind, quickening my pulse. Your ass was powerful, like two great smooth rocks sculpted by the sea. "And the swimming clears my head," you went on, your voice unchanged, putting on your briefs. "Entirely. It's like I'm bathing my mind."

I asked you what you needed to clean from your mind as you pulled on your trousers and turned back to me, your dark hair falling over your forehead.

"Different things. Work. The future. And you? What clears your head?"

"Reading," I said without needing to think.

"Oh yeah? What are you reading right now? Anything good?"

I couldn't bear to look at you while I thought. The sky had turned an even darker blue, and I felt safe in the dimming light.

"Right now, nothing. But I'm starting a new book soon, and I think it'll be really good." I thought of *Giovanni's Room*, hidden at the bottom of my bag, its precious pages waiting to be read.

"What's it called?"

You sat next to me. I looked at you, the air in my throat suddenly immobile and heavy, my mind reeling. I didn't know why I'd let myself bring up this secret, tried hard to think of another title to tell you. The distant sound of the camp bell rang through the air, stirring us both. Then an odd silence between us, like something balancing on an edge, deciding which way to fall.

"It's dinnertime," you finally said, rising. "C'mon. I'm starving."

We walked to the camp, back through the fields, the light fading. I felt peculiarly close to you, and happy to have you all to myself with nothing but the sky looking at us. I asked where you had learned to swim so well, and you told me that there was a river not far from your house, where you had played with your brothers. You said that they had taught you.

"And in the summer we'd go around the mountains and swim in the other rivers there," you said.

"Where?"

"Near Rabka. By the Tatra Mountains."

"A southern boy," I said, smiling.

You nodded. "Can't you tell from my accent?"

"Now that you say it, yes." Some of the words you said, even later, were inflected with a drawl, pulling the last syllable out like pliable dough.

"And you?"

"Wrocław."

"A city boy, huh?" Your eyes flashed in the dark.

By then we had reached the camp. We stopped in front of the canteen, as if we'd agreed on it before.

"See you tomorrow," you said, putting your hand on my shoulder for a moment and then going in, leaving me standing outside.

That night I took *Giovanni's Room* out of the deepest recesses of my bag and started reading it by torchlight after the others had fallen asleep. It scared and comforted me—even just the first few pages. The narrator's guilt toward his fiancée, his desire for Giovanni, and the deep regret for whatever it is he did to him. There was something about the rhythm, the language, about the knowledge implied and the sense of internal doom, that spoke directly to me. This wasn't distraction or entertainment: here was a book that seemed to have been written for me, which lifted me up into its realm and united me with something that seemed to have been there all along and that I seemed to be a part of. It felt as if the words and the thoughts of the narrator—despite their agony, despite their pain—healed some of my agony and my pain, simply by existing.

I lived through the narrator for the next few days, thinking of his life during my work in the field, suddenly knowing that there was a place for me to go that was mine, which was completely my own. As soon as work was over, I changed into my clothes, grabbed the book, and walked out through the gate, but not to the spot where I knew you'd be. I wanted to be by myself for a while. I found a place by the river, in the other direction, shielded by thorny bushes, and there I'd lie on my back and sink into Baldwin's world.

One day, when I'd only just settled down to read, a shadow passed over the page. I turned around and saw you standing behind me.

"So this is where you've been hiding," you said, sitting down beside me. You looked at the book, which I'd quickly shut and set on the ground. "So, it must be very good, then."

I couldn't say anything; I couldn't even nod.

"What's it about?"

My heart started beating fast.

"It's about a boy," I said, trying to keep my voice steady. "An American who lives in Paris."

You looked at me expectantly. "*And?* What's he doing in Paris?"

"He . . . He's trying to figure out what he wants, and how to choose for himself."

You looked at the cover. "Can I see?"

I handed it to you, regretting it immediately, as if I'd handed you something heavy and dangerous. "Why is it glued between other covers?" you asked, eyebrows furrowed.

I shrugged. "It's sort of unauthorized, I guess."

To my surprise, you laughed. "I didn't suspect you of being such a rebel," you said, handing the book back. "Can I read it when you're done?"

My stomach dropped. "If you want to."

"Yeah, I want to. I've never read an underground book."

"Really?" I smiled, feeling pleasure, an ounce of power. "I would have suspected you of being more of a rebel."

It surprises me that I shared the book's existence with you so early. But I felt a strange trust there by the bank. There was something about the way you looked at me that made me feel as if you didn't judge. There are only so many people we meet in life who give us that feeling. And yet that night, as I lay in bed reading after the others had gone to asleep, I was scared. Scared about the hole I had made by trusting you, scared by the vulnerability it had created. And the more I read, the more scared I became: the immensity of the truth and the lies I'd been telling myself all those years lay before me, mirrored in the narrator's life, as if someone were pointing a finger at me, black on white, my shame illuminated by a cold, clear light. In the brightness I could examine it with almost scientific clarity, and suddenly the narrator's pain didn't soothe my pain anymore. His fear fed my fear. I was like him, David, neither here nor there, comfortable in no place, and with no way out.

When I went to dinner one night, the book left hidden under my pillow, the duplicity of my life—both who I was inside and who I was to others—struck me as surreal. The book and you had brought it hurling back, and I decided never to be that vulnerable again, never to feel that panic again, never to depend on anyone else. So I avoided your eyes when you walked past our table that night, fixed my eyes on the bloodred borscht instead. And I didn't come to the river in the days that followed. The end of the camp was in sight. I stayed in the hut and read and avoided you, hoping the days would slip by unnoticed and I could just go home to my old life. During the breaks in the field, I'd sit in the shade, leaning against the boards of the wooden toolshed while you'd join some of the guys by the water pump, smoking, joking with them, trying to catch my eye. I pretended I didn't see.

By then the uniform had adapted to my body, yielded to its shape, and my body had adapted to the land. We knew what we were doing now, and all one could hear for most of the day was the thud of the beets falling into baskets. The mountains of them grew more quickly, until there were almost no rows left. At one point, during the last week, I was working away, lost in the repetition of my movements, when I saw you standing above me. You looked like you'd been there for a while, watching me work.

"Did you finish reading the book?" Your question sounded like a challenge.

"Yes," I said, into the earth, feeling my jaw clench, continuing to work.

"Do you still want to lend it to me?"

I stopped digging. My heart was galloping. I looked up at you, and I don't know what made me do it—maybe it was the sincerity with which you asked, which was drawn on your face, or maybe it was a sense of resignation—but I nodded. I decided I had nothing to lose. Our paths would never cross again, and I didn't want to be like David, afraid of himself and devoured by regrets.

"I'll bring it round to you at dinner," I heard myself say.

That night I waited for you by the canteen exit, in the half-dark where people smoked and gossiped before they went to bed. I waited for you until late, until the streams of people leaving had dried up and I thought I had missed you. I was thinking about returning to my hut when finally you came through the door. The girl was right behind you. She looked poised. Her eyes, like her hair, were dark and intense, but her skin was light, pale even, as if she hadn't been in the sun at all for all these weeks. You exchanged a look with her that I couldn't see, and then she glanced at me with a vague smile and walked off into the dark.

"I read quickly," you said, slipping the book into the back pocket of your trousers.

"Don't worry about it," I said, feeling sadness wash over me. "You can keep it."

You looked at me like I'd said something absurd. "What are you talking about? Of course I'll give it back." Then you put your hand on my shoulder again, just like you had done the second time we'd talked. And just like then, the knot at the bottom of my belly—home to both fear and desire—stirred like an incoming tide.

That last week did not, as it usually does, pass more quickly than all those before it. It crept to an end on all fours. All throughout the week, I wanted it to be over, wanted to be liberated from being around you in that state of uncertainty. I still avoided you, still never came to the river, even though it was hot and I longed to dip my feet in the coolness of the water. And yet I kept looking at you when I was sure our eyes wouldn't meet, to see signs of any change in you. But you seemed the same. In the canteen you sat with the same group, and in the field you worked incessantly.

On our last evening the comrade leader made a speech, thanking us for our hard work. Then he ordered us down to the river. We walked in little groups, unsure what would happen, filled with excitement tinged with dread. But what we came upon were dozens of little boats flopping in the water. We got in, six to a boat, me with Karolina and Beata and the boys from my hut, and we rowed down the river, not toward our spot but in the other direction, where the forests began. We formed a line of boats with Belka at the head. We saw the sun set far behind the fields we'd so carefully emptied that month, and along a narrow arm of the river that snaked its way into the forest. Tall pine trees began surrounding us, fragrant, solemn, and seemingly infinite. It was cooler there, and utterly dark, and soon the only light came from the faint moon above us, barely visible in between the canyon of the treetops and the distant light of Belka's torch in front. We heard the sound of light paws on the forest floor and the cracking of branches. An owl hooted.

Then our convoy stopped, and we all got out. There was a clearing in the forest. A fire was made that threw light on the ground and warmed us in the cool of the night. Sausages were pierced on twigs. Someone took out a guitar and began to sing, and bit by bit that wild dark place turned intimate. The night was full of noise and crackling and talk. We stood by the fire and drank beer, and the boys talked about their trip to Romania. Farther off, in between some trees, I saw you standing with your group: the girl with the dark hair and Maksio Karowski. I observed you for a moment, your profile in the dark, the way you smoked your cigarette, holding it between thumb and index finger. Then I forced myself to look away.

Toward the end of the night I was sitting by the fire by myself, sipping a beer and staring into the flames. I was thinking about the rest of the summer, the rest of my life, and struggling to see anything. It seemed like the only thing that was certain was change itself, unstoppable and careless like fire eating wood. Then a shadow moved and you sat down on the log beside me. We didn't say anything for a while. I felt weak. You looked exposed in the light of the flames, and even more handsome, with your red-and-black-checkered shirt, your eyes reflecting the fire. You looked around, as if to see whether anyone was listening. There were many conversations around us, couples dancing, others sitting on logs, singing along to the guitar.

"I've almost finished the book," you finally said.

"And?" I tried to sound detached as my pulse began to quicken.

You looked into the fire. "I like it. I can see why it's not officially published."

Our eyes met for a moment, and you smiled.

"Why did you stop coming to the river?"

I turned my head away. No words came to me. Finally I looked up and saw you looking at me with tenderness.

"Don't be scared."

The way you said this—softly, perfectly calm—pierced right through me. The flames crackled. I nodded; that's all I could do. You smiled, dissolving the tension, your teeth flashing in the light of the fire. We sat there for a while, in our private silence, worlds shifting in me.

"I'm going to the lake district tomorrow," you said. "I've never been, and I always wanted to go. And I thought this was the moment, before returning to the city, before real work begins. There are some great places out there. Lakes, rivers. I have a tent and all." You paused, and our eyes met again for a moment. "I've been meaning to ask you: Do you want to come with me?"

CHAPTER 3

I REMEMBER THE BUS LEAVING with the others, and you and I staying behind. It was an overcast day. Rucksacks on our backs, hands around the straps, we walked up the country road, hoping to hitch a ride. I was nervous and we talked little, but somehow the silence between us was a pact. I felt like a small bird set loose, scared and exhilarated by the void before me.

The first car that stopped took us east. The driver, a middle-aged man, eyed us from time to time but asked no questions. We drove silently along country avenues lined with tall chestnut trees, past fields bordered by poppies. I had no idea where we were. We had no map and there were few road signs, but even if there had been more, the names of the places would have meant nothing to me. While I took it in, this nameless expanse, you slept with your face against the window.

At some point in the afternoon the driver let us out at a country junction. You tore a coupon from your hitchhiker's booklet and passed it to him.

"Hope you send it in and win a hair dryer or something!" you cried, and swung the doors shut. He nodded and sped off into the horizon.

A strong, humid wind blew into us. The sky was filled with black clouds, and the air felt electric. Then, as if someone had pushed a button, rain started to fall. There was no maybe, no in between. It poured without any inhibition, drops heavy like paint, a million of them, and us caught in the middle of the road with our bags and no umbrella.

"Quick!" you cried. "Over there by the tree!"

I followed you, sprinting across a field, our clothes already darkened from the rain. We reached an oak and sat down by its trunk, protected under its roof of leaves. The rain continued to hammer the land, and the world smelled of water and earth. Then lightning struck before our eyes—a devil-fork of neon-white on the dark horizon. Thunder followed. We watched the spectacle in silence and awe, pushing our wet hair out of our faces, arms clasped around our knees. For a long time we sat like that, staring into the sky, until the rain became softer.

"Don't you wish sometimes you were somewhere else?" The question came to me out of nowhere.

You turned toward me. "You mean the West, don't you?"

I nodded, surprised by my candor. I'd never talked to anyone other than Karolina about this.

"No," you said flatly. "Why?"

"I don't know. I've always been curious. It seems like everything is better there. More beautiful. More free. Don't you think?" I looked at you hopefully.

You shook your head and stared at some distant point on the horizon. "I should have known you're one of them."

"Them what?" I said, nervous suddenly, wondering whether I had made a big mistake.

You turned to me briskly. "Dreamers," you said, your mouth widening into a teasing smile.

I let the word ring out, relieved and warmed by your smile

so close to my face. "What's wrong with dreaming about free-dom?" I said.

"*Freedom?*" you huffed, and smiled, as if you'd had the same conversation many times before. "Having oranges and bananas every month of the year—is that freedom to you?" Your smile was gone.

"There is freedom in having what you want," I said carefully, "in choosing for yourself."

Your eyes narrowed. "And do you think that doesn't come with a price? You think these people in the West don't spend their lives working like machines, earning just so they can spend?"

"I don't mind hard work. As long as you get something for it."

"It always seems better somewhere else," you said, ignoring my comment. "There are so many chances here. Look at me"—you seemed to blush a bit here, lowered your eyes for a moment. "I come from a poor family. And I'm the first one to get a proper education. They even gave me extra points in my entrance exams because we're working class. And now I'll work for the government. This is freedom. I could have never had that un-der capitalism. The Party cares about us. When my mother got sick"—you swallowed, your voice becoming smaller—"they sent her to a sanatorium for three months. *Three months.* Do you think they give that to anyone in the West? For free?"

I shifted, adjusting myself over the thick roots of the tree. "But don't you care that *we* are not really free? They tell us what they want us to know, and that's all. We're not even allowed to leave the country when we want to. We're being *kept.*"

You were very calm, didn't say anything for a while. "You're making it sound worse than it is," you finally said. "And how do you know it's really better anywhere else? Ultimately, we've got to work with what we have. It's as easy as that." You smiled and looked at me. "See it as a game—everyone knows the rules. And if you can't change them, there's no point in worrying."

A cool wind started to blow, and I felt a shiver, goose bumps on my arms.

"But maybe we *can* change them," I said, feeling foolish suddenly, reaching for something that was no longer there.

You smiled lightly. Your complete lack of worry surprised and relieved me. "To answer your question . . . It would be nice to go and see it one day. The West. But not as an escape. I'm not like David in *Giovanni's Room.*" You smiled again, and a rush went through me. "But I'd like to see something else. 'Cause you need to try things out and see them for yourself, right?" You slapped my knee and heaved yourself up. "C'mon, dreamer, we've got to get going now, unless you want to sleep out here on this field."

The rain had stopped, and everything around us was quiet. The sun came out, faint and ready to disappear behind the horizon. We walked down the road with our thumbs stretched out, but no cars stopped for us. We walked and walked until the sun set, and we still hadn't gotten anywhere. The fields around us were wet from the rain, not ideal for camping, and we didn't know what to do. Finally we found a farm where a family agreed to put us up for the night. The farmer's daughter showed us the barn, where they allowed us to sleep. She brought us bread and lard, which we devoured like wolves. Then we spread out our sleeping bags on the hay beside each other.

"Good night," you said after you'd switched off your torch. You undressed without a trace of self-consciousness, your silhouette in the dark crawling into the sleeping bag next to mine.

I could hear you breathe, like a gentle crashing of waves. And slowly, drop by drop, the rain started up again. It pattered on the roof like fingertips practicing piano chords. We lay on our backs and listened, not saying a word. I sensed you near me, your body somehow animated despite its stillness. My heart was beating faster than the rain. Suddenly I wanted to be close to you, desperately so. I could feel the pull of your body, little strings drawing me toward you. But I couldn't move. Heartbeats passed, light years of back and forth in my mind, and just when I began to think I would never have the courage, you shifted toward me and placed your head on my shoulder. My heart stopped. I didn't dare breathe. Your head was heavy, like warm marble, and your hair brushed my cheek. I was paralyzed by possibility, caught between the vertigo of fulfilment and the abyss of uncertainty. I thought of how rashly I'd acted with Beniek that night so many years earlier, at the dance, when the lights had gone out. How painful and unforeseeable the consequences had been. Despite that, I had just gathered the strength to think about what it would be like to touch my hand to your hair, that it was the only right thing to do, that now wasn't then, when you whispered, "Good night, Ludzio," and shifted away from me. It was the first time you had called me that; you'd changed my name affectionately. It made the void on my shoulder even more unbearable.

"Good night," I replied weakly, turning around, regret washing over me. Your breathing became calm and steady. My mind raced like a crazed horse. The rain carried on through the night.

When I woke in the morning, I saw your body rising and falling peacefully with your breath. Through the cracks between the wooden boards, strips of light entered the barn, illuminating you. Your shoulder was covered in little freckles I had never noticed, random and beautiful, like a constellation of stars.

I climbed out of the sleeping bag as quietly as I could, pulled on my T-shirt and shorts, slipped on my sandals, and went out into the morning. It was a clear day, and the sun was already up, soft and new like a freshly peeled egg. The air smelled green and yellow and deep, fertile brown. In the daylight the farmhouse was smaller than I remembered, only one story high, made from dark wood with a steep roof of old brown tiles. It looked both ancient and fragile, as if it had stood in this place forever but might easily be crushed. Just outside it, the farmer's daughter was feeding a group of chickens. She was about fifteen, with a bright, heart-shaped face and a timid, childlike smile, and she was wearing a headscarf. She greeted me and invited us to breakfast.

"We're in the kitchen," she said. "Come and bring your friend."

I went back to the barn and found you up, pulling your trousers over your tight, white briefs.

"Hey," I said, aware of my forced voice.

You zipped up and turned around. "Hey." You looked almost shy, ran a hand through your hair.

"Hungry?" I asked.

"Starving."

We walked out of the barn and into the house. There was a dark corridor that smelled of must and soot and earth. Nothing seemed to be moving. A few beams of light revealed a world of dust specks floating in the air, and on the wall Jesus hung on a cross, muscles and ribs defined, naked but for his loincloth. We looked at each other for a moment, quizzically, suddenly close again in the dark. Down the creaking corridor we found the kitchen on the right, where the young girl stood by the stove over a pot of steaming milk. She'd taken off her headscarf, and her long dark-blond hair fell all the way down her back.

"Come and have a seat," said an old woman by the table in the corner. "You must be hungry."

We sat on wooden chairs that creaked under our weight. Everything felt as if it had been covered in dust, worn out by generations of use. The plates were chipped and glued back together, the motifs on the cups faded. Faint, pearly light came from a small window.

The old woman looked us over shrewdly, curiously. "My husband is out," she said. "Help yourself." It dawned on me that she wasn't so old after all and that she wasn't the girl's grandmother, but her mother.

We started to eat. There were cucumbers and radishes, a pot of honey, and a hunk of bread. The daughter came over from the stove and poured the hot milk into our cups.

"So you're students," the mother said.

"Yes, ma'am," you said through a bite of radish, looking more at ease than I felt. "Just finished our studies."

She nodded, as if she was agreeing to something uncertain. "Married?" she asked, looking at you.

"No, ma'am," you said, shaking your head, smiling at her. "Not yet. Am still young."

She laughed in her hoarse voice, revealing a set of missing front teeth. "And you?" she said, turning to me.

I could feel myself blush. "No, ma'am." I took a sip of milk to hide my discomfort. My lips brushed against the floppy skin that had formed on top, sending a wave of nausea through my belly, and the liquid scalded the inside of my mouth. I tried to keep a straight face and reached for the bread.

She watched us eat with apparent satisfaction. "So you're traveling. Know where you're going?"

"Just looking for a quiet spot," you said. "Can you recommend anywhere, ma'am?"

She looked out the window, where nothing much of the outside could be seen, only a hazy green from the trees and a vague blue of the sky. "There is a place not far from here where we go and pick mushrooms in the autumn. Travelers don't know about it. It's pretty." Her eyes sparkled, and in one moment I saw, really saw, that she had once been young. "I'll tell you how to get there."

After breakfast, we rolled up our sleeping bags and packed our things.

"Just walk, about four miles straight through the forest from the Marianki junction," the woman said, standing by the entrance of the house. "You'll know when you've arrived."

"Thank you. You've been very kind," I said.

She took my face in her solid waxy hands and kissed me drily on the cheek. "Come and see us on your way back. Have a good trip."

In a nearby village we found a small truck going in the right direction. The driver was bringing a load of cherries up north, and the only space he had for us was in the back, in the mountains of fruit. We ate beyond hunger. Stuffing our faces, staining our hands, we spat the pits into the passing fields. The sky was infinite and light; it felt as if we were flying through it. Almost every farm we passed had a stork's nest on the roof, with the elegant creatures atop, resting or flying off to look for food after their long journey from Africa.

We drove without stopping. We passed people working their fields with their carts and horses, men and women and children with large wooden hoes. Wild flowers and high yellow fields met the blue sky, and then the land became flatter and the first *cerkwie* came into sight, the first Orthodox churches, black and small and mysterious with their bulbous domes. They signaled a different land, the beginning of the wild and unaccountable east, where kings used to hunt for bison and where the plains are infinite. The driver stopped at an almost invisible crossing, stuck his head through his window. "This is it, boys." We jumped off and found ourselves standing at the mouth of a pine forest.

"Are you sure?" I asked.

He nodded and wished us good luck, then drove off, leaving a cloud of dust behind. We looked at each other, hesitating.

"Are we sure about this?" I said, suddenly aware that it was just you and me again, nervous like on the first day I'd met you.

"What else can we do?" you said calmly, smiling. "Let's go." You put your hand on my lower back and pushed me with you into the forest, sending a shock of warmth through my body.

There was a narrow path, just like the woman had said. We walked into the sea of pines. Inside it was cooler and darker than in the heat of the sun. Side by side we walked on a bed of dried needles the color of cinnamon. The previous night floated on the surface of my mind like a buoy: the rain on the roof, the weight of your head on my shoulder. I tried to shake it off. You were wearing the same white linen shirt as the day before, dried overnight, cherry-stained, unbuttoned to reveal your collarbones, the dark halos of your nipples guessable beneath the fabric.

As the forest grew denser and thicker, the sky seemed farther away and the sunlight barely reached us. But the small path, made by the feet of those who'd walked before us, was always there. You walked ahead swiftly, and I followed. We didn't speak, and you never turned around to check whether I had fallen behind, as if there were a thread attached between us.

"They were nice, weren't they?" I said at one point to fill the silence, to cover my thoughts.

You nodded, without turning round. "Yes. They were."

You seemed as deep in thought as I was. We walked on, and the trees became less dense; the sun trickled through again. And not long after, in the distance, we could see the forest ending, something shimmering there. We quickened our steps, almost ran then. As we came to the last rows of trees, we saw it: a clearing filled with a large, brilliant lake, lined by high grasses like a secret. We moved closer, my knees weak with discovery. The water's surface glistened in the afternoon light, a deep, calm blue. There was not a soul around. We walked to the edge and let our bags drop to the ground, looking across the lake, gleaming like a mirror hit by midday sun. The forest was all around us, and we were in its center, protected and soothed by this glittering eye.

"We have arrived," I whispered.

You nodded.

"She didn't promise too much, that old woman!" Your cry was sudden, jump-starting you into action. You stripped off your clothes, abandoned them one by one until you were completely free, the white of your ass contrasting with the brown of your back, jumping in with a scream that echoed across the clearing. You reemerged with a triumphant smile.

"You coming?"

First I slipped off my sandals, then my shirt, which I folded carefully and laid on a soft spot on the ground. I took off my shorts, and then, with a flicker of hesitation, my underwear. You had turned away, swum a little way off. I stood there feeling the wind graze my chest, tickle me between my legs. I looked at the water. I couldn't see through its body, couldn't assess its contents. But I stepped in. And the water embraced me completely, softly and coolly. I felt myself anew, as if something in me had been switched on after a long time. It was a sensation of lightness and power and total inconsequence. I began to move, and every movement propelled me forward. The sky above was lighter than the water, specked with tiny clouds. I was conscious of the unknown underneath.

"See, you can do it!" you screamed from across the lake, ecstatic.

I was calm.

My body moved in your direction, and you looked at me, suddenly calmed too. With your arms outstretched to the sides, you were like a ballet dancer hovering in flight. Under the surface of the water something warm rattled in my belly. I approached, until I could see the drops of water on your forehead and on the tip of your nose and in the corners of your mouth. We didn't say a thing. We looked at each other, already beyond words. You were there, and I was there, close, breathing. And I moved into your circle. All the way to your waiting body and your calm, open face and the drops on your lips. Your arms closed around me. Hard. And then we were one single body floating in the lake, weightless, never touching the ground.

That evening, as the sun began to set, we pitched the tent underneath a large pine. It was still warm and the lake had turned black and cicadas sang calmly and there was no light anywhere but the thin slice of moon. We lay down on our sleeping bags. Wind blew softly against the tent, and the only sound was that of the tree above us swaying along, its needles rustling and whispering to themselves. We lay on our backs, hands folded beneath our heads, our elbows touching lightly. Through the flap in the tent's roof we saw the sky filled with stars. They were tiny and there didn't seem to be many, but the closer you looked, the more there were. You could never hold on to all of them. Looking at them made my head spin warmly.

"I'm glad this happened," I said, enjoying the sound of my voice and its gentle vibration in my body.

"Me too." You turned your head toward me, your eyes bright. "I knew it would happen since the beginning," you said, smiling.

"Oh yeah?"

"Yeah. When you looked at me that first day, when we arrived. You're easy to read."

I laughed and pushed against you. "Oh yeah?"

You smelled of water and pines. There was softness, and there was hardness. I could sense your tan under my fingertips, and with your strong, solid hands you drew me afresh, creating me, the small of my back, my inner thighs . . . and you. Your back, your chest, your stomach, your thighs, your cock. Hard and impossibly close beneath the softness of your briefs, caressing my palm, obvious, world-shattering, demanding. We moved fervently, struggling. There was so much I could not get enough of, so much I would never be able to grasp or possess, no matter how much I tried. And I tried, we tried. Covering ourselves with each other, merging into one, pulling, following the pull, letting its current take over. Our sighs were shared, refused to release us. The night reminded me of the Easter bonfires I would watch as a child in the park nearby, where the pyramid of wood burned from top to bottom, chasing the ghosts of winter, bringing a thaw, releasing the warmth from the dormant, the resting. The flames would hypnotize me. I'd merge with them, with their dancing, destroying, and bearing. We played this struggle, breathless and elated, heads light and filled and spinning, until exhaustion, until we released ourselves onto each other and fell asleep entangled like weeds.

I don't know how many days we stayed at the lake, because each one was like a whole world, every moment new and unrepeatable. In a way these felt like the first days of my life, as if I'd been born by that lake and its water and you. As if I'd shed a skin and left my previous life behind.

The lake and the forest became our territory. We fished, making rods from branches and using bits of bread as bait, and we grilled the fish—flat and gray and delicious—over the fire and ate them with our fingers. We walked into the forests behind the lake and found berry bushes and small clearings the size of living rooms, where branches hung over beds of white flowers. We'd lie down and make love, falling asleep afterward. We'd wake in hazy happiness with the sun still above us, and when we'd walk back to the tent, the only thing we'd leave behind was the shape of our bodies in the flattened grass.

The lake cleaned us every morning and evening. It washed

off the sweat of summer and of lovemaking, maybe even the fingerprints on our bodies. And every time I swam I experienced the same elation I'd felt the first time I stepped into the lake, devoid of struggle, a feeling of weightlessness I hadn't thought I could feel. During these days the shame inside me melted like a mint on my tongue, hardness releasing sweetness.

I floated in the water, and you lay by the shore reading *Giovanni's Room*. The air was the same temperature as our skin, or a little lower, caressing us. Later we'd lie next to each other and watch the clouds, observe the change of their fantastic shapes: from unrecognizable to familiar, familiar to unrecognizable.

One afternoon, toward the end of our stay, we went to the nearest village, about an hour's walk away. We found a small shop and bought bread and cucumbers and apples and beer. The sun was descending as we made our way back. It was dark before we reached the forest. You'd forgotten your torch. The path was lit only by moonlight. And as we walked along the fields, the image of my childhood nightmare returned to me, like a challenge from the past—the empty silence of the world, the fields stretched out on all sides, a sense of the monoliths staring back at me. But I didn't even have to decide whether or not I was scared. I wasn't. The tombstones—along with the shame—were a mere memory, dissolved like sugar cubes in summer rain.

We walked on through the forest, taking in its furtive sounds, until we reached our clearing and saw the moon on the surface of the lake. We stopped and watched. Then, without a word, we undressed and slipped into the water. We swam, fearless and free and invisible in the brilliant dark.

CHAPTER 4

NIGHT FELL PARTICULARLY EARLY today, and outside the city glimmers across the other side of the river like a sequined dress of steel. I was hungry when I got home and decided to make a sandwich. The bread is white and already sliced. Over here, all you have to do is chew. I buttered the bread and sprinkled sugar on it. It's not the same as home, but it did the trick. Then I picked up the phone and dialed Granny's number. The signal was still busy. I've been trying for days. I tried not to worry and wrote her a letter instead, asking how she was. Of course they will open and read it before she does. But I no longer care.

After that I switched on the TV. The news is getting worse: they're hunting down the opposition, arresting the key figures of Solidarność, dispersing the underground, hunting down trade union leaders. Probably torturing them, said the presenter, her pretty face matter-of-fact. I believe it. I don't want to, but I cannot help myself. I wonder: Are you involved? That's the question that follows me around like a shadow. Would you still defend the Party now?

Maybe the worst thing is that I have no one to speak to, no one who could open the window on this stale air of speculation. I know that, eventually, I will need to find someone to trust. At the office they ask me how I am every day, about a dozen times. It took me a while to understand why they were so baffled by my attempts to answer, to understand that my answer isn't the point. That *asking* is. So now I say that I'm fine. I even attempt a smile. But I sense that either way my foreignness somehow absolves me from their judgment. To them, it must explain my strangeness completely.

———

When I was still a child, Mother and Granny would lock themselves in my mother's room every evening. I never knew what they were doing in there, and they never allowed me in. Whenever I asked, they'd say that I wasn't old enough to know.

"And you mustn't tell anyone we do this," Mother would say, crouching down to my level and placing her large, hard hands on my shoulders. "You understand? No one. If you do, something bad might happen to us." Her face was tense, the deep worry lines above her brows making her look spent.

"Are you doing something bad?" I asked, scared.

"No, my darling." Her voice mellowed. "But even when you don't do bad things, bad things can happen to you."

"Why?"

She tried to look soft, but the lines on her forehead didn't disappear altogether. "This is how it is."

They wouldn't say anything more, no matter how much I begged. I would put my ear to the door, but all I could hear was a very low sort of crackling, indistinguishable voices. I couldn't see anything—the keyhole was filled with the key. Much later they'd emerge from the room talking in urgent, hushed voices, sometimes sad, sometimes almost joyful. And though I was used to their nightly ritual, it still frustrated me to be excluded from its secret.

The day I learned that Beniek and his family had gone, my mother came home and found me in my room, wrapped into myself, crying. She must have known this was serious because I didn't cry often, and when she asked me what the matter was, tears choked my words. She sat on the bed, and I put my head on her lap, the material of her skirt cool against my cheek, her arms around me. I continued to cry, encouraged by her comfort, letting the tears out until there were none left. She stroked my hair, and when I had calmed down, I told her I had gone to see Beniek, how that strange woman had opened the door, and what the lady from church had said.

"Why did they leave?" I asked. "Will they come back?"

I could see indecision in her eyes. Before she could speak, Granny appeared in the door, as if she'd been listening all along.

"I think he is old enough now," she said, looking at my mother gravely. "He needs to know."

Mother looked from her to me, silent for a moment. "Ludzio, you won't say anything, will you?"

I shook my head, suddenly jerked out of my sadness. She looked at her watch. "Come on, then." We went into her room, where Granny closed the door behind us and shut the window and drew the curtains. It was still light outside, and children were playing hopscotch in the street below, hopping and skipping across the pavement.

"First of all, you need to be quiet," said Granny, pointing at the wall we shared with the neighbors. "And don't ask any questions until it's over. Just listen."

She walked to the dresser and lifted the protective cover off the radio, revealing its compact body, the dark, smooth wood glistening in the light. We placed three chairs around it and sat down. Mother pushed the black button and carefully adjusted the indicator. At first there was nothing but a low crackling. Then there was music, a flute playing a jolly tune. Then the music ended, and I could feel Mother's and Granny's bodies tense. A voice began to speak:

"This is Radio Free Europe, broadcasting live from Munich, West Germany. News at 8 o'clock. Monday, the twenty-first of June 1968."

The man's voice was different from the voices that usually came out of the radio. It was calmer, less aggressive. He wasn't shouting or proclaiming. Mother and Granny sat frozen, their hands holding up their chins and covering their mouths. I tried to concentrate like them, but I didn't understand much of what was said. He used many words I didn't know, acronyms that meant nothing to me. It was like another language. At one point he mentioned *"Israel,"* those jagged syllables that had become so potent in only a day. I tried to guess the meaning of it all but only saw blanks. When the program was over, Mother moved the indicator back to another station and turned up the volume. This, I discovered, is what she would do every night, so no one would ever know they had listened to the forbidden station. And while the music played, they began to explain. They explained about the Jews, that there had been many in Poland before. For a thousand years. That most had been killed in the camps that the Germans had set up during the war. Granny recalled seeing her neighbors forced onto trains, never to be seen again. Of course we weren't really taught this at school. We were taught that the Germans had suppressed the *Poles* and how our Russian brothers had saved us. Jews weren't Polish, of course. Some Poles still blamed them for the war. That year, Mother said, there had been unrest, student strikes all across the country. So the Party had turned on the Jews. They had called them traitors, dismissed them from their jobs. This was why Beniek's family had left. Once they were gone, no one ever spoke about them again. One day your country is yours, and the next it isn't.

Beniek's departure spelled the end of my childhood, and of the childhood of my mind: it was as if everything I'd assumed before had turned out to be false, as if behind every innocuous thing in the world lay something much darker and uglier. Every evening now Granny and Mother would let me into the little room. We'd huddle together by the speaker, silent and serious, leaning forward, listening to the voices from across the Wall, and after the program was over, Granny and Mother would explain something new about our history. How for over a century the country had been divided by Russia and Germany, how it had ceased to exist on the maps. How our culture had survived in the underground, parents teaching children their forbidden language and history, and how the country had finally gained independence after the First Great War. They taught me about the second one too, the side we were never told. How, after years of occupation, the people of Warszawa rose up against the Nazis, how the Soviets arrived, and how, instead of helping the Uprising, they stayed on the other side of the Wisła and waited. They knew they'd win the war, knew the Germans would retreat eventually, so they let them take revenge on the Poles. The Soviets watched on as the city was decimated and its population slaughtered or deported. When the Germans finally left, there were fewer than a thousand survivors in the capital.

I guess you believed what they told us in school, that the Soviets were our liberators. That they were the good ones. Our allies. Sometimes I wish I could have been as light as you. Because I didn't enjoy those nights in my mother's room, those terrible truth-spills. They were a ritual, their pull too strong to resist. Even if I didn't understand it all, I understood enough for anger to collect at the bottom of my stomach. The fact that I couldn't tell anyone made it all worse. I'd been handed a poisoned gift, powerful truths I could never admit to knowing. Mother had made me swear never to mention anything to anyone, lest they sack her—or worse.

I suppose the scariest thing was the lack of certainty. The fifties were over, and people no longer disappeared for speaking out. But in the sixties—and even later—things were more arbitrary. Almost anything was possible, depending on who happened to denounce you and what they thought they could get from you. Even with my childish intuition I sensed that a single mother was more vulnerable than most.

So, just like before, I'd take part in the morning salutes at school, and bow in front of the portrait that hung above the teacher's desk, of Party Chairman Gomułka's ancient, crumpled face scowling down at us. I took part in the marches, in the parades, in the May 1 celebrations, the anniversaries of the October Revolution. Holding banners with obsequious slogans praising our Soviet brothers, singing the songs they had taught us. I was like the little boy in Hans Christian Andersen's tale "The Emperor's New Clothes," except I didn't speak up. I pretended not to see the obvious truth: that we had never asked for this system. That it had been forced upon us. I sat through the lessons and endured it all, carrying Beniek's banishment inside me, bile collecting in the pit of me. During breaks I'd pick fights with other boys, coming away with a bloody nose or busted lips and temporary relief. And I swore that I would never become one of them, of those who led their mendacious lives in submission to the system.

———

One day, as you came out of the lake, you asked me whether I had a girlfriend. I shook my head, thrown by your question. You were bent over drying your thighs, and I couldn't see your face. I smiled to hide my embarrassment, even though you couldn't see me.

"No," I finally said. "And you?"

You'd reached your feet. I watched you run a corner of your flimsy towel through the crevices between your toes. Then you looked up, confident that I was waiting for you.

"No," you said carefully. "Not really."

"What does that mean?"

You straightened, brushing your hair back with a hand. You looked both defiant and amused.

"It means I used to. But not anymore. I prefer *this* now."

And before I could ask anything further, before I could gauge your words and the corridors lying beyond them, you came over and pulled me in. Your mouth set down on my neck, avidly. *Like a vampire,* I thought, and closed my eyes.

On the last morning at the lake we packed our things and dismantled the tent. We watched it collapse onto the ground like a dying hot-air balloon. Then we flattened and folded its lifeless body and pushed it into its cylindrical bag. We did it all without exchanging a word.

"You know we can't tell anyone," you said to me, suddenly serious, pulling the bag closed.

"About what?" I asked. I knew exactly. My stomach was like a towel being twisted. I watched you collect the rods lying scattered on the ground, opening the bag again and shoving them inside.

You threw me a furtive look. "About this."

I picked up a stick and threw it toward the lake, seeing it fly and fall in vain, not making a sound.

"No. I guess we can't."

We hadn't really talked about "us," or what it would be like back in the city, or anything else. There was no "us." Of course, I had thought about it, had wanted to ask: "What *is* this? What are we going to do with it when we get back?"

But I never asked in the glare of daylight—I wouldn't have dared. Maybe I'm confused, the moments merging into one another, disfiguring one another like too many voices speaking at once. But now that I think of it, I remember I only dared ask on the last night, as we lay in the dark of the tent, about to fall asleep after having made love. I asked the question into the dark, afraid. You didn't say anything for an interminable moment, and I thought you had fallen asleep. Finally, you whispered, "I don't want this to end."

My heart beating hard, knocking against the wall of my chest, I replied: "Me neither."

When we arrived in the city, light came from every corner, bounced off every facade as hotly and radiantly as I felt flooded with happiness and anxiety. I was no longer in control. I'd think back to the lake, the tent—compulsively, like the birth of something I could not yet imagine. I had found my place on your sandstone body—between your thighs and the mounds of your nipples, in the cave of your armpits. The geography of you was suddenly as clear as that of the city, skin warmed like the bricks of the tenement houses, the lines of your body like the straight and unbroken lines of the avenues, of the tram tracks and the stiff metal barriers that threw crisscrossed shadows onto the streets. The same barriers that appeared stable but could move under your weight, creaking when you leaned on them for too long, threatening to release you onto the busy car-ridden tar.

When I arrived in the flat, it seemed smaller to me than before. The kitchen was to the right, as soon as you entered. It was long and narrow and only big enough to hold my landlady, *Pani* Kolecka. This was her territory. No matter how scarce the supplies, no matter how harsh the rationing, she was always in there, baking. Somehow, there would always be sugar and flour and something she'd scrape up or exchange. There'd be *szarlotka* apple tarts or *babeczka* cakes with cream, or layered gingerbread with plum jam. She baked like her life depended on it, and maybe it did. I had loved her ever since I'd moved in, fresh from Wrocław, referred from the center for student accommodation. I loved her warm voice and her soft presence and her small, childlike face. She seemed so old it almost made her ageless, like a being from another world. Usually she'd sleep on the brown couch in the living room, next to the table where we ate and the cabinet with the collection of rocks her husband had left behind. But in the summer the block heated up like a glasshouse, and sometimes, when I got up at night to go to the bathroom, I'd see her sleeping there on the tiled floor of the kitchen with the door open, large and peaceful, like some creature swept up by the sea.

The door to my room was next to the rock cabinet. It held a foldable bed and a small desk one pushed aside to open the door to the balcony. We were on the seventh floor. All you could see were the tops of the other blocks, like the heads of people standing in front of you in a crowd.

You and I lived on opposite sides of the city: me to the west, you to the east, and separated by the Wisła. A tram connected us, passing through the Old Town and across the river. To the south, always visible, the gigantic Palace of Culture towered over the rest of the city.

I lived where the Ghetto had been, where the Nazis had razed everything to the ground to leave no trace of their crimes. Wola was the name of the neighborhood, "Will" or "Determination" in English. The Party had rebuilt it as part of their socialist dream. A network of identical blocks stood lined up neatly like cardboard boxes, as far as the eye could see. We called this the *blokowisko*. There were new parks, new trees, and new children, playing obliviously in between the blocks on layers of invisible footprints and the dust of forgotten lives.

You lived in Praga, one of the few neighborhoods that had made it almost unscathed through the war, where the Russians had waited and watched the destruction of the city by the Germans, where they had looked on without firing a bullet as the Germans destroyed Wola. As they quietly and clearheadedly decimated the Old Town, the museums, the libraries, the archives, allowing a whole world to burn into oblivion.

In the first weeks back, Warszawa was empty and hot. We walked the bright avenues and bought berries and sunflower heads from the old ladies and ate them at the Saski Gardens near me, by the hill with the white pavilion. We stopped at milk bars. We ate cool *chłodnik* soup, the sour milk and pink beetroot soothing our throats. We drank fruit *kompot,* which colored our tongues, and for dessert, noodles with melted butter and raspberry jam. Later, full and content, we'd lie in the high grass near the zoo in Praga and watch the sky through the gaps in the solid branches of the trees above. Our words, our stories, poured forth like springs. I told you about Mother and Granny and even about Father. How he'd left us when I was very young, how I could barely remember him. How I barely wanted to. He'd moved to Kalisz and never visited, and all we saw of him were the meager alimony payments the postman brought every month. Mother always said he'd never wanted children, that he'd wanted her all to himself to love and control.

You listened, really listened, gentle eyes taking me in without judgment, making me feel more heard than I knew I could be. Then you told me about your family in the mountains. About your brothers, whom you had looked up to as a boy and who'd become "nothing," drunks like so many others, passing out every payday, whose bodies the police picked up from the benches and pavements and left overnight in the sobering cells. You talked about your parents and their work in the sawmill. How ignorant they were of you. "They hardly know what this means," you said, looking around at the city. "I want to show them. They can be proud of me." You told me about your job, starting a week from then. "For the Office of Press Control," you half-whispered, as if pronouncing the name of a god. A shiver ran through me, made me forget it was summer.

"You mean the Office of Censorship," I said, despising you for a moment. "The ones who ban the books we need the most."

Irritation flickered across your face. "Don't be such a square. Everyone's got to start somewhere. You have a better idea?"

"Let's go away," I said, surprised by the boldness of this. But you only looked amused.

"Where would you like to go? Rome, Paris?"

"I'm not joking, Janusz."

"You know what, Ludzio? You're a crazy one. Look around you." We were protected by the high grass, the sun shining on us. "Why would we leave all this?"

That evening we climbed to the top of the Palace of Culture and saw the city lying before us, its vastness suddenly tiny, its end—the chimneys of the factories and the forests behind the last houses—a secret resolved. The Wisła snaked itself through the middle and continued on, beyond the human-made structures, toward the mountains in the south and the sea to the north. The mist of the day's heat dissolved above the blocks. Summer was at its height; time was suspended. And I never wanted it to run again. Like a dice, spinning and spinning without ever coming to a standstill.

The weeks passed, and I hadn't seen Karolina since the camp. I decided to visit her. She rented a room from a crane driver in Żoliborz, in the far north of the city, the only part Bowie had ever seen, when his train stopped on the way from Moscow to Berlin, just a couple of years before you and I met. It made him write "Warszawa," a terribly desolate song. But Żoliborz isn't the worst neighborhood by far. It's residential, made up of 1930s Bauhaus-style flats, a run-down garden city. There are trees everywhere, large and oblivious, and carpets of grass occupy every space between the gray buildings. In summer, it's a two-colored world—gray and green. But, of course, Bowie saw it all in winter, when there is only one color left.

I knocked on Karolina's door. The crane driver opened it, wearing curlers in her hair and a dressing gown around her barrel-like body. She knew me, although she never showed any sign of it. With a dry "good morning" she led me along the corridor, which was decorated with empty packets of Western cigarettes (Camel, Ambassador, Marlboro) arranged on a shelf. She led me toward Karolina's room at the far end of the flat and knocked on her door before I could. Her curlers shook in her short hair.

"Miss Patocka," she cried, "another man for you!" She threw me a satisfied look and walked off. The door opened, and Karolina's face appeared, breaking into a smile.

"Ludzio, it's you." She kissed me on both cheeks, her blouse soft against my bare upper arm. "Come in, close the door."

She walked across the room, picking up clothes that were lying strewn on the floor, the chair of her desk, the bed, and pushed them into a wardrobe in a corner.

"Never mind the mess," she said, throwing herself onto her bed and looking at me wide-eyed. "I didn't expect you. But I'm glad you came. Sit." With her palm she tapped the space next to her. I obeyed. "I hope she wasn't too mean?" She looked at the door and rolled her eyes.

"She hasn't become any more refined."

"Did you hear how she tries to humiliate me?"

"As if *that* could humiliate you—another gentleman caller."

She smiled, her coral-colored lips stretching over her big teeth.

"So, how have you been?" She looked at me for a moment, as

if reading me. "You've changed," she said calmly, like a clairvoyant announcing someone's fate.

"Have I?" I made a grimace.

"Your face." She held her hand to it, her middle finger resting on my cheekbone. "It looks like something's opened up, something that was folded tight. Like a fist. I'd never noticed it before, but now I do."

"You can save your wise words for one of your gentleman callers." I laughed, gently pushing her hand away. "I'm the same."

She shrugged, getting up from the bed and sitting down at her desk, which also functioned as her dressing table with a mirror on the wall. A photo of Isabelle Adjani was tucked between the mirror's frame and its glass, a still from Polanski's *The Tenant*. Adjani looked rapt behind an enormous pair of tortoiseshell glasses, hair big and frizzy, ring-covered fingers seductively placed by her lips. Karolina picked up a pair of tweezers and started plucking an eyebrow. She was sitting with her back to me. In the reflection of the mirror she looked startled and concentrated, her gaze moving from her brows to the photo to me. "Don't make me pull every word out of you individually—what was it like with him?"

She never called you by your name.

"Good," I said, shrugging, trying to sound as natural as I could. "We camped by a lake. Swam, fished. It was fun."

"Mmmh." She ran the tip of her ring finger along the brow she had been working on and moved on to the other. "I had no idea you two were friends." She sounded absentminded, but I sensed her disinterest was feigned.

"He asked me on the last night, in the forest," I said, shrugging. "And we weren't really friends. He had no one to go with and I had nothing to do, so I thought I might just as well."

She stopped what she was doing, and her eyes moved over me in the mirror. "You know you can *tell* me," she said softly. Her words ran through me like a string pulled tight.

"There's nothing to say," I said, looking at her for a moment and then turning to the window. There was a silence, and in its space I tried to decide whether my sudden anger was with her or with myself, for being unable to speak the truth. Through the door we heard a radio playing, a marching band blasting out a tune with insistent joy.

"What's new with you?" I made myself ask.

"Me?" She continued plucking. "Your friend here got herself a job."

"What? That's great."

She set down her tweezers, took a cigarette from a packet on the desk, lit it, and quickly blew the smoke through her nostrils. The tips of her fingers were blackened from the soot of her cheap Romanian Snagovs. "As a secretary to some asshole in the Ministry of Justice." She sounded like a judge announcing someone's prison sentence, matter-of-fact, a little gleeful.

I was taken aback. "What about the placement? Weren't you going to train with the divorce lawyers?"

"No spaces." She blew out smoke with her head lowered, staring at the carpet. I could see her eyelashes pointing toward the floor. "Turns out I had no chance of getting anywhere without connections, whatever my grades. Who was I fooling anyway?" She sighed, lifting her head. Her sad eyes grazed mine for an instant, and then she turned her head toward the window. "But maybe it's better that way, I don't know. Maybe I would have hated it. I might apply again next year."

I nodded, tried to seem encouraging. "Yes, you will. This is just temporary."

She nodded, as if she were trying to believe me.

"So what's it like?" I asked.

She shrugged, took a deep drag. "I only started last week. Don't ask me what they actually *do* in that office. I get the councilor his vodka in the morning and type up a letter or two in the afternoon. Other than that he treats me like a showpiece for his colleagues. He asked me to wear my tight sweater more often. So much for my four years of higher education."

She took an ashtray from her desk and crushed the half-finished cigarette. "I smoke too much," she muttered, placing the ashtray on the table, trying to smile at me.

"Come here." I patted the empty space beside me on the bed. She obeyed. Her head sunk onto my shoulder, and I slung my arm around her. We sat like this for a while, seeing ourselves in the mirror, searching for something in our own reflections. "I'm sorry," I whispered finally.

"Oh, don't be. It never turns out the way we think it will. And anyway, I was one of the lucky ones. At least I have permission to stay in the city now that we've graduated. Otherwise they would have sent me straight back to Tychy, and God knows what I'd be doing there. Living with my parents." She straightened and tried to laugh. "I'm just not sure I'll be able to take it for long."

"You won't have to," I said. "I'm sure of it."

"Yeah?" There was doubt in her eyes, a need for reassurance. I nodded and took her into my arms. Her body was like a furnace. I almost felt like I was burning myself.

"It swallows up all your thoughts, all your self-respect," she said, with a note of despair I had rarely heard her use. "I can already see myself becoming one of those bitter office ladies."

"You won't become one of those," I said, taking her by the shoulders and looking her straight in the eyes. "I'll make sure of it. Not while I'm alive."

She smiled and released me. "See, you *have* changed," she said. "You've become an optimist."

She stood and walked over to the window. Branches of blindingly green leaves rocked in the breeze, slowly, peacefully. She opened the window and stood there for a moment, looking out, breathing in deeply.

"And you? Have you figured out what you will do with yourself, Ludzio?"

"I've had some time to think this summer," I said, hyperaware of my voice. I was looking at my hands, assembling my words. "I think I'll try for that doctorate after all. You know, the one Professor Mielewicz said I should do."

She turned around slowly, her face immobile. "*Really.*"

I shrugged, meeting her eyes for a moment. They were hard and vulnerable at the same time.

"What made you change your mind?"

"I thought about it again. The allowance from my father will run out soon, and I have to do *something*. This might be better than rotting away in some school or library, no?"

"You once said you'd rather work in a factory than sell out."

I bit my lip. "Well, that wasn't true, was it?" I said, trying to smile.

"And what about the topic? What if they make you write about what they want?"

I shrugged again, harder. "I'll find a way around it. Or not."

She nodded, turning back to the window, putting her hands on the sill. I got up and joined her there.

Beyond the branches, in the houses across the street, clothes hung from lines strung outside the windows: the fabric of people's lives drying in the sun, swaying with the wind. Large dresses in faded reds and mustard-yellow, shirts with stiff collars that resembled obese men whenever a gust of wind filled their interior, towels rubbed down over the years. In the street, girls in knee-high white socks had drawn boxes on the ground with chalk, were counting and singing, jumping one-legged along the potholed sidewalk.

"I was serious when I said we can always leave," she said, lifting her head toward me. "You know that, right? My uncle in Chicago could find us something. Or we could book a bus tour to Germany or France, and just get off and run away." She smiled, somehow sadly.

"There's no need to rush into anything," I said, feeling the weight of her stare. "We always said we'd try our chances here first. Maybe things will get better."

"Nothing ever gets better here," she said, closing the window and walking back to her bed.

"We don't know that yet."

"Do we not?" She looked at me with curiosity. "I guess you still need to find that out for yourself."

The next day I walked to the Old Town, along the New World Promenade, Nowy Świat, past the cafés and busy shops, past the church where Chopin's heart is buried in a pink marble column and where the students rioted in 1968 and were beaten by the police. I walked through the iron entrance gate of the university, into the faculty grounds. It was strange to come here in the middle of summer, before term had begun: empty lanes and empty lawns and the large shade-giving trees with no one underneath them, the library deserted but for a couple of researchers. The peace of the place took me aback. I felt like a ghost as I passed through the literature department, the corridor that echoed every single one of my steps, and knocked on the thick door that read "Professor Mielewicz." I could hardly believe it when my knock was answered with a "Come in." As usual the professor was sitting in his armchair, surrounded by stacks of books, papers piled before him like the unsteady skyscrapers of a conjured-up city. He was a round man of about fifty, with dark hair he combed back over his large head, an affable expansive face with round glasses.

"*Pan* Głowacki, what a pleasure to see you." He said this calmly, as if somehow he'd known I'd come that very day. "Have a seat." He closed the book he was reading, slipping a pen between the pages. "You've come because of the doctorate, isn't that right?" He smiled knowingly.

I nodded. "Yes, Professor."

"You want to do it, then?"

He looked at me intently, almost too directly. It made me feel see-through.

"Yes, Professor," I said, this time a little less assured.

"Good." He smiled and leaned back, taking off his glasses and rubbing his eyes as if he was wiping something away. "You know what you're getting yourself into?"

I hesitated. "Not really, sir." He laughed, deep and bearish. "But I want to try."

"That's the right attitude." He leaned forward and put his chunky arms on the desk, his fingertips touching one another. "Because I cannot guarantee anything, you see. Ultimately, the board needs to accept your proposal, and they're a tough bunch." He turned sideways in his chair, bent over, rummaged in a drawer. Finally, he pulled out a thin stack of papers. "Here, fill these out. And bring me a proposal by the end of the week. We'll look it over together."

Before he handed me the papers, he threw a careful look at the door, then back to me. He spoke with a lowered voice, a sort of thought-through whisper.

"I need hardly tell you what the conditions are. Something that won't be too upsetting, you see." He made a wave-like gesture with his hand. "Nothing controversial. Nothing remotely anti-socialist, no whiff of pro-Westernism, my dear. Recently they've been getting increasingly nervous about that sort of thing."

"I understand," I said, taking the papers from him.

We shook hands, and I turned to leave.

"And, Ludwik?"

I turned back around. He was looking at me with almost paternal concern.

"Make sure it's good. All right? There are other candidates. I want you to get this."

I nodded and left his office, shutting the door behind me with trembling hands. Standing in the empty corridor, I let out a deep breath.

I walked home slowly. The air was suffocating. The sky was gray, and sticky wind blew through the streets, swirling up dust. The few people around looked hurried, caught inside their own minds even more than usual, their faces like masks. I was relieved to get home. *Pani* Kolecka wasn't there. I sat and took out the papers the professor had given me. My head was empty, but I started anyway, placed pen to paper. I forced myself to think. I didn't really want this, but neither did I want to let it slip away. I had nothing else, no other path. And there was a certain pleasure in doing what I had not allowed myself before, a satisfaction in the forbidden, a challenge. I knew what I really wanted to write about, the book that had moved me more than anything, more than any book before. But I also knew I couldn't write about *Giovanni's Room*. It had never been published in Poland. I wasn't even supposed to know about it. But I had read Baldwin's other stories. They dealt mostly with the black man in American society, of his discrimination and shunning. I could see its relevance, could see how it exposed the double standards of the West, how it showed racism and white supremacy behind the liberalism and democracy extolled by the capitalist powers. At the same time, of course, I could identify. I carried my difference, my shame, on the inside. It wasn't visible—not to everyone straightaway, at least—but it was there, and it was a danger. That's what I began to write about.

I remembered what I'd read about Malcolm X, about his friendship with Baldwin, and his struggle, his radical views on oppression and self-defense. I wrote furiously, my body dissolving, my head spinning, losing all sense of time.

The keys turned in the lock, and *Pani* Kolecka stood in the door. I was struck by how short she was, how dwarfed by the size of her shopping net, which I took from her and placed on the kitchen counter.

"Thank you, dear," she said, removing her beret. "The queues are getting longer. Or my legs are getting weaker. But I managed to get meat." She smiled her small smile that came through her eyes. "It's a miracle."

A moment later potatoes were boiling, and I sat at the table, grating carrots.

"Let's be happy," she said, taking the meat out of its stained gray paper and placing it on the counter. "If things continue this way, any *kotlet* might be our last." She started beating it with a prickly mallet, the banging almost drowning out her words. "You heard the news?" She handed me a dry white roll, a plate, and started to crack open eggs on the edge of a bowl. I shook my head.

"Gierek decided to increase the meat prices."

"What?" I looked at her in disbelief.

She turned to me, wiping her hands on her apron. "Meat products are up by sixty percent in the canteens."

"They can't just do that," I said, disbelief mingling with anger.

She turned back to the meat, beating it again with her mallet. "That's what we thought before. But they can, and they will."

Later we ate without speaking, savoring every mouthful, the *kotlet* with its crispy breading and the grated carrots with cream and the buttery potatoes sprinkled with dill. Usually, *Pani* Kolecka would tell me stories of her life and her marriage, her travels with her husband, how she had accompanied him on his expeditions. But not that night. That night something hung over us. One by one, in the night outside, the lights went on in the *blokowisko*.

Your house, like all the others in Praga, was tired and beaten down. Bullet holes shaped like stars covered the facade, and rusty balconies faced the street, some with clothes hanging to dry. Beyond the arched entrance was the courtyard, where, surrounded by high grasses and yellow gladiolas, stood a Madonna.

Her face was pale, and she wore a blue gown, palms turned up to the sky, a halo of gold-painted stars around her delicate head.

In those days, I was as far away from the church as I would ever be, but there was something about the beauty of this statue, in the midst of the courtyard's decay, that moved me, stayed with me as I walked up to your flat. The stairs looked so old and fragile I wasn't sure they would carry me. They smelled of dampness and groaned with each step, but they held. On the first floor an old woman looked at me suspiciously, ignored my greeting. On the third floor a band of children ran across the landing, screaming and cursing like drunkards. Your place was on the fourth and last floor.

"Ludzio," you whispered when you opened the door, throwing a searching glance at the landing behind me.

Your room was small, but you lived by yourself. That in itself was luxury. Old wooden floors, two fragile windows facing the courtyard, a desk, an iron-framed bed in the corner where we lay down. We kissed for a long time, hard, trying to still a bottomless thirst.

You asked whether I was hungry and fished out a loaf from behind the curtains, pulling them shut. You cut the bread, holding it against your chest like a baby and moving the serrated knife toward your heart. We sat there for a while, chewing with satisfaction on the fat slices, hearing the creaking sounds of the house and the muffled voices of the neighbors. I told you how I'd shown my idea to Professor Mielewicz that day and how excited he'd been. The proposal would be ready for submission that week.

"That's great," you said between bites, your eyes glistening. "I hope you get it."

"Me too," I said. "And if not . . . I don't know what I'll do then."

You turned to me, seemingly encouraged. "I could try to get you work in my department once I'm settled."

I shook my head. "No." You looked at me, as if expecting an explanation. For a moment, neither one of us spoke. "Did you hear about the food prices?" I finally asked.

You nodded and looked away.

"And?" I probed. Now the silence was yours.

"And *what*?" You shrugged. "If they do it, it needs to be done."

"Are you serious? They are doing it because they don't know how to run the country. Where do you think all our food is going, all the food we produce? It's paying debts. It's going to Russia and to the West. And we have nothing left."

You were quiet for a moment, your face frozen. "You need to watch who you say this to. You know that, Ludzio, don't you?"

I held your stare. "But you know it's true," I said, determined.

You got up, retrieved a half-empty bottle of Mazowszanka from under your desk, and poured it into a glass. "Yes." You said this quietly, with your back to me. "But there's no good in knowing that. None at all." You returned to the bed, handed me the water. "For your own sake, don't be so hotheaded. Or you'll get yourself in a lot of unnecessary trouble."

"So why don't we—"

"Let's drop it," you said abruptly, your tone striking me with its sudden coldness. "We haven't had the same lives. We won't agree on this."

My head was reeling, the glass cold in my hand. You had never spoken to me like this, with such detachment. I didn't know whether I wanted to run away or be appeased. Either way,

I no longer felt like talking. A new silence took hold and began to scatter your last words, to cool their vehemence. You lay on the bed, staring at the ceiling, and I lay down beside you. Then your hands found their way to me, your eyes meeting mine consolingly, blinking an apology. Our bodies moved toward each other by instinct. I felt your chest underneath your shirt, retraced the swing of your collarbones, the hardness of your shoulders. You tasted the same, warm and earthy. I pulled off your clothes in the dim light. Your tan was still visible, and around us the house was alive—feet shuffled below, water pipes gurgled, taps were turned on and off, accompanying our struggles. Later, when night had fallen and we had exhausted ourselves, we lay facing each other, the tip of your nose on the bridge of mine. Nothing else mattered in the dark.

"I'm starting my job tomorrow," you said after a while.

"I'll come and pick you up if you like."

You shook your head. "Better not. Better not give them a reason to suspect. I'll meet you at the pool. On Wednesday."

I said nothing, letting your words echo in my mind, weighing them individually. "So we've suddenly become a secret, huh?"

You lifted yourself on to your elbows, your eyes looking darker.

"We've always been a secret, Ludwik. It's just that until now there was no one to hide from." You smiled for an instant, maybe out of discomfort. "Do you know what they would do if they found out?" Your brows furrowed. "They have lists. They keep track. And they know how to use information." You let your index finger pass across my cheek, gently. It felt like a threat. I flicked my head; your hand moved away.

"There's no law against what we're doing."

"I know that." Your voice softened. "But we need to act as if there were. Do you know what they did to Foucault?"

I looked at you blankly. "The philosopher?" You nodded. "What's he got to do with us?"

You sat up on the bed, your back against the wall. "He came to Warszawa when he was young to head some French cultural institute, and the Secret Service knew about him. So they found a handsome student and introduced him into Foucault's circle and made sure the guy charmed him. It worked. One day the two of them took a room at the Bristol and *boom*"—you snapped your fingers—"in come the agents, catching them in bed. They charged Foucault with soliciting prostitution. A week later he'd resigned and was back in Paris." Your voice sounded almost triumphant, as if impressed by their efficiency. But for an instant I saw a wavelet of anxiety ripple across your face. "You see?"

I said nothing. The water pipes churned with a low thud—still or again, I wasn't sure—and I felt a heaviness settle over me.

"And you want to live like that, Janusz, in fear?"

You laughed, your confidence in place again. "I'm not afraid. We just need to mind our own business. Avoid risks, be smart. As long as we do that, we'll be fine. Don't you think?"

I shrugged, feeling defeated.

"Good." You jumped up from the bed, newly energized. "I'm going to take a shower." Slipping on a shirt and shorts, you disappeared into the corridor.

That week you started your job and I worked on my proposal, submitting it to the board after some help from the professor. Then all I could do was wait. And because the flat was small and my nervous energy overwhelming, I spent my days walking through the city. One morning I walked through Wola, past the *blokowisko,* toward the cemeteries. The largest was the Powązki. It had pruned elm trees and endless rows of graves with crosses, all cared for and dusted and attended to like sculptures in a museum. Next to it was the small Muslim cemetery for the Tatars that no one ever seemed to visit. It was the size of a classroom, with the graves beginning to disappear in the grass like an archaeological site in the making. And then there was the Jewish cemetery. It was large and deep, a rectangle with no visible end; no one could look inside. It was abandoned, gates locked forever. The only thing I could see was the army of giant poplars soaring above the wall that separated—protected—the city from this shard of history. I walked along that wall, its old red bricks covered in vines, and admired the sturdy trees swaying in the wind. I imagined nature taking its course on the other side, the little forest growing from the hearts of forsaken graves. From where I stood, they looked like the most beautiful trees in the city.

I walked on, passing the abandoned factories, where flocks of crows lingered and cawed with their chalky, swordlike beaks, throwing large shadows across the dusty plots. Crossing Wola and going toward the center of the city, I reached the square with the monument to the Ghetto Uprising. I shivered as I took in its size, the pain of the distorted faces carved into its facade. I quickened my pace along the large wide avenues. You could only cross every five hundred meters, and it made you feel both exposed and removed. I walked and walked, across the Feliks Dzierżyński Square, all the way to the center, then a little south toward the Palace of Culture and its gigantic spire that pierced the late-summer sky. Standing beneath it—Stalin's gift to the city, its concrete knot, its biggest scar—I looked up, and my head began to spin. It was September, still warm, yet somehow the air already contained a hint of decay.

I walked home. The city had filled up again after the emptiness of summer. Students had returned for another year, workers had come back from their holidays. The queues for the shops swelled like bloody lips—deliveries had become so few and far between that the only way to get anything was to wait. The lines had started to occupy whole streets. I had to push through a queue for a grocery store, where women stood with empty baskets, trying to look over the heads of those in front to see what was happening. Sometimes they stood and talked, but mostly people kept to themselves, mumbling complaints, telling off those suspected of pushing in.

Pani Kolecka would go out every morning, early, and join the queues that seemed most promising, according to a rumor picked up by some acquaintance. She would walk the city, carrying shopping nets in her handbag at all times, and whenever she chanced to walk past a queue that seemed as if it might yield something—whether it was toilet paper or canned beans— she'd join and wait.

Most evenings *Pani* Kolecka came home empty-handed, tired. She'd sit at the table in the living room, her hands illuminated by a tiny lamp, using leftover cloth to make hats she'd sell in the queues. She'd smile at me when I got back from your place, night having fallen outside. "Waiting for nothing, queuing for a possibility, that's what we're all doing now," she said, quietly, one night. Her eyes sparkled with sadness and irony. "There is no other currency than time. And it's cheap."

We were eating less, and fewer things. I often ate at the

campus canteen, though not the meat. But sometimes we'd be lucky. Sometimes I'd come home and she'd be standing in the kitchen, the radio beside her playing Chopin, something fragrant cooking on the stove, most likely with cumin. She loved cumin.

"Come and eat, Ludzio," she'd say, with a smile in her small eyes. "You must be hungry. Sit down and tell me about your day."

One morning, while I was still waiting to hear from Professor Mielewicz, I found *Pani* Kolecka lying on her bed in the living room, a blanket pulled up to her chin. "It's the standing," she said, coughing. Her cough was dry and violent, like a complaint. It seemed strange that a small, fragile being could make such a sound. I prepared some tea for her, dissolved honey in it that she'd brought from the countryside where her sisters lived. But it didn't help. The coughing continued. "I'm sorry," she said, her eyes red with exhaustion. "I will need to get some medicine."

That night the winds grew stronger, the trees in the court-yard moved against one another, air howling between their branches. I woke up and heard the coughing from the next room, sharp and uncontrolled, like a threat.

The next morning, I went to the pharmacy for *Pani* Kolecka. They didn't have what she needed.

"We might get it in two weeks," the pharmacist said, without a trace of emotion on his face. I tried another pharmacy farther away, and they told me the same. I walked back to the flat with anger collected at the bottom of my stomach, pulsing through my body.

"Don't worry," said *Pani* Kolecka. "I'll be fine. I just need some rest."

I made her some more tea and boiled some vegetables. I brought her food from the canteen, *ruskie pierogi* and pickled cabbage. But the cough continued. Its dry, cracking sound would stir me from sleep, accompany my nights. As if something was trying to tear up her body from the inside.

During those weeks, you and I would go to the university pool every now and then. It wasn't far from the Old Town, tucked in below the ramparts of the faculty grounds. I remember its large reception hall and the strong smell of chlorine—how I liked that smell—and the cloakroom where we left our shoes in a shared cloth bag. In the changing rooms we undressed among other boys, drying themselves, joking around, unaware of their nudity or used to it like something that was a given—strong backs and thighs and asses, skin smooth and covered in drops like forest leaves after rain. But in a strange way that didn't excite me. When we were naked like that, changing, showering among them, we weren't really ourselves. We were lighter, without consequence. We took off our roles along with our clothes and only belonged to the anonymous world of bodies. And when we swam our rounds and I pushed through the water, I felt even lighter. It reminded me of our summer together, of the ease with which we'd floated across the lake. As I swam I dissolved in the water, and something came to me from the depths of my memory.

I was very young; Father had just left us, and Mother was so distraught I was afraid she'd die from grief. She stayed in her room all day. Her lips pale, her eyes red. I tried to cheer her up, to distract her with my picture books that I'd bring to her bed and read out loud. And one day she came out of her room, her face made up, lipstick on and eyes dark with kohl, and she took me outside and lifted me onto her bike. We rode all along our street and across the large empty park to the pool in the domed Centennial Hall. This is where she taught me. This is where we went into the water together, and she, my lifeline, held me while I wriggled my legs and arms, exhilarated and free. She taught me patiently to trust my body, to let myself float, to move on my own. For years we'd go together, even when I no longer needed her to hold me. I wanted her to see me, to be proud of me. To make each of us feel important to the other. So when the day came, some years later, when they found something in her lungs and I came home from school to find the flat empty, with only Granny crying on the couch, it never occurred to me to go back to the pool. Not without her. It was as if that part of my life had died along with her, as if it could never return.

One night, after one of our swims at the pool, it was beginning to get dark outside. Coming out with our hair still wet, we could see the Wisła shimmering, the trees moving slowly in the wind. The air smelled fresh and moist. Summer still lingered, but already one could sense the cooler winds sweeping across the endless plains from Siberia, announcing the end of warmth. It was autumn's gateway, that night.

We wandered down the slope of a little park and onto Dobra Street. It was the first time I'd seen you after you'd started work, and you told me that your boss liked you. That he'd already given you texts to read: books awaiting permission to be published. It was your job to examine them, to find criticism of the Party or anything unsuitable for the public. You seemed electrified, your eyes wide, your words sounding like they were meant for an audience.

I let you go on, unsure what to do with my anger, until you stopped your speech and looked at me.

"Have you nothing to say?" you asked, as if expecting praise.

I let silence rush in, hoping it would blur the reality of this moment. Our footsteps resonated in the dimly lit street. There was no one there except us. I held on to the stillness for as long as it would let me, for as long as I could.

"You should know by now that you will never impress me with your work," I heard myself say. "That it will never bring us closer." You looked as if you were about to say something. "Meanwhile," I went on, unable to contain the bitterness, "the queues are becoming infinite. There is less and less to eat. And *Pani* Kolecka is ill. She's coughing like a death-bound dog. They don't even have the medicine for her."

Your face lost its tension. It was your turn to be silent.

"I'm sorry," you finally said, sounding reduced, speaking only to me again.

"I'm sorry too. I'm sorry to be living under this bloody system."

Your brows furrowed, and you glanced behind us. "Don't *say* things like that." There was a hint of fear in your voice.

It gave me a strange satisfaction. "What else are we going to do? Let them do anything they please?"

You stopped, looking behind us again, grabbing me by the shoulders. "Work. Keep quiet." You looked straight into me. "Don't do anything stupid." I avoided your eyes. "I mean it, Ludzio." You shook me, as if trying to wake me up. "I told you we mustn't take risks. You want to protest? What for? To end up in prison and to be a martyr for nothing?" I raised my eyes and looked at you, suddenly aware of us standing like this in the street, our faces so close. "There are ways to live a good life," you went on, as if hearing my thoughts. "I'll figure things out. Can't you trust me?" Your eyes pleaded in a way I had never seen before. We heard the sound of boots clicking on the pavement.

"Janusz?" A cry came from the other side of the street. A girl was standing in the round spot of light streaming down from a streetlamp. "Is that you?"

You released me. "Hania!" Your face lit up.

She crossed the street, and you fell into each other's arms. I saw her face on your shoulder, smiling for a moment with her eyes closed. My mind reeled. She opened her eyes and looked at me. It was like seeing a ghost—the pale, white skin, the intense, dark eyes. I'd never seen her up close, but I still recognized her. It was the girl I'd seen you with at the camp. She looked very stylish, in a trench coat and cowboy boots. But even more remarkable were her earrings: they were beaded and shone in all colors of the rainbow, like the tail of an exotic bird, and so long they almost touched her shoulders. I couldn't take my eyes off them.

"Janusz, I haven't seen you in ages," she cried, adjusting her hair, making the earrings move along with her. "Where have you been all these weeks?" Her eyes fell on me. There was a pause in which she and I looked at each other, slightly embarrassed, until you said:

"Here, let me introduce my swimming colleague. Hania, this is Ludwik."

We shook hands. Hers was soft and white like a dove.

"It's a pleasure to meet you," she said, sounding like she meant it, looking into my eyes for a moment before turning back to you. She put her hand on your arm.

"I'm going to see Rafał now—he lives just around the corner. Do you want to come?"

You glanced from her to me. She was entirely turned to you.

"I would like to, but—"

"You're *busy*?" She raised her eyebrows. "C'mon, just for one drink. We've been saying how much we've missed you."

I could see your fingers closing tight around the strap of your bag. You wore an expression I found impossible to read.

"I can't tonight," you finally said. "I'm sorry. Next time."

She looked at you for a while, until a smile curled itself around her lips. "Fine. But no excuses for my birthday party. At the end of the month. You're coming. Yes?"

You nodded. She kissed you goodbye and ran off, her boots beating on the concrete. We stood for a moment without speaking, the air strangely charged. You looked gloomy, worried even.

"Everything OK?" I asked.

You nodded, without looking at me. "All good. Let's go."

"Do you think she saw us?"

"I don't know. I don't think so." Again your face was inscrutable.

We climbed a set of narrow stairs lined by a large stone wall. Behind it lay the nuns' convent, their cloister with its orchards and grazing cows, and new residential blocks towering just above.

A group of boys in tight jeans came toward us, walking down the narrow passageway. One held a small, heavily made-up girl around the waist, while another, with a sharp face and gelled-back hair, looked you up and down with curious eyes. You noticed him, and your face seemed to harden; you looked away. We reached the top of the bridge and waited at the traffic lights. To our right lay the city, the neon lights of the tall buildings glistening, advertising clubs and restaurants, to our left the Wisła and the dark shore of Praga. I thought I could sense your restlessness. You looked at me from the side.

"What is it?" I said.

You looked ahead, at the red light. "I think it's better if I spend tonight by myself." You sounded careful, circumscribed. "Just tonight."

"Why?"

"I need some time alone."

I looked into your eyes, trying to discern what this meant. Your look was steady.

"I'm just tired," you said. "I need to rest. All right? I'll see you soon."

"Is it because of Hania?"

You shook your head, not looking at me. "Don't overthink it."

The light turned green, and a tram appeared. We said good night, our hands in our pockets, and then you crossed over without turning back.

Three days passed and no message came. Rather than drive myself crazy, I caught a rattling tram to the other side of the river. You opened the door shirtless, holding a razor in your hand. You seemed surprised to see me but not displeased. You invited me in. There was a water bowl on your desk and a little mirror propped against a pile of books.

"I'm just getting ready to go out," you said, sitting down and running a hand over your stubble. "A drink. My boss invited us to his place." You tried to sound casual and threw me a glance as if to test my reaction. I was calm. You took up the razor and looked at yourself again. "Can we see each other tomorrow? At the pool?"

I nodded, relieved to have some certainty. "Sure. Have fun tonight." I managed to say this without sounding sarcastic. You stood and kissed me hard on the mouth, razor still in hand.

I went to a student café near campus and prepared for my interview with the board that would take place if I passed into the next round. I'd come to like my topic on Baldwin's analysis of racism in America. Professor Mielewicz had praised it too, saying I'd be the first in the country to examine it. It made me think that throughout my life, up to this point, everything I'd done had felt either irrelevant or replaceable. Here, for the first time, was something wholly mine, something that needed me in order to exist. I was expecting news from the professor any day now. I tried to remain hopeful.

When the café closed, I took my things and made my way home. It was a balmy night, maybe the last one of the year, and so I decided to walk, taking the long route. I walked toward the Old Town, where the lights had been switched off for the night. Couples sat kissing at the foot of King Zygmunt's Column or leaning against the walls of the reconstructed castle. I walked through the little narrow streets, past the cathedral, and out onto the old market square, which was almost empty except for some tourists taking photos of the restored baroque facades. The sky was a square, drawn by the high roofs of those houses. And then I heard the faint but steady sound of a saxophone, with a bass chasing after it. The melody drifted through the air, little more than a whisper of jazz.

I walked toward the sound on the other side of the square.

The music seemed to come from a darkened building with all its curtains drawn. One ground-level window was illuminated. I crouched and looked down into a vaulted cave filled with a buzzing crowd, smoke gliding from their faces toward the ceiling, glasses held to their lips. A band was playing just below the window. I recognized the composition as one by Komeda, maybe from the soundtrack for *Knife in the Water*—tempting, chaotic, then languid. My mind listened to the story of the notes as my eyes wandered the crowd until they landed on you.

It was as if someone had turned off the music, like an electric shock in my mind. You and your perfectly shaven face, turned toward her, her earlobe between your fingers. Her long earrings reflecting the light in all the colors of the spectrum. A rush went through my belly like a snake. You moved together to the music, you holding her and her holding you. Her hands were on your shoulder, her painted fingernails flashing in the light, her long skirt shifting with the music. This is an image I cannot forget: your hands around her waist, your fingers sinking into the fabric of her skirt. They looked settled there, and I was struck by the tenderness in your eyes. I watched you both as if you were a pair of strangers. I tried to tell myself that it didn't mean anything, that it wasn't real. And yet I could no longer look at you without feeling absolutely drained of any power. I got to my feet, feeling light-headed, my vision blurred for a moment. I walked home, my heart beating twice for every step I took.

———

I guess you never knew that I saw you that night. Do you remember the music? Do you remember her earrings? Are there things you've forgotten or things I've missed out? My memory has its limits, of course. It may color in the blanks without admitting to it, dramatize or revise. I guess there is no photographic memory for emotions. But this is my truth right now, for better or worse.

I left work early today. The flat was a mess, so I tidied up. Here it is beginning to grow cold, but it's still mild for the season. In the mornings it's best to wear a coat, but the midday sun is strong, and on the avenues of Midtown businessmen take off their suit jackets during lunchtime, their white shirts glistening in the winter light, their gym-trained asses pushing against the fabric of their trousers as they move purposefully down the street. Not like at home, where by now people must be wrapped in scarves and hats. I bet the air is already sharp, stings your face. I remember that cold, the merciless crisp cold of Warszawa in December. And for a moment it feels as if I am there among the smell of diesel and burning coal, the long broad avenues with the Palace of Culture looming over us, you beside me. Of course I still see them here, the Poles, in the streets of Greenpoint, buying their poppy-seed cakes and *pierogi* and *twaróg* cheese. I spot them a mile off. So easily. Like recognizing like. But the ones that come here are different—they have hope in their eyes, just as I did when I arrived. They are awake.

I switched on the TV at ten o'clock. A speech by Reagan, images of some space shuttle, Muhammad Ali falling to the ground in the ring. Then the image behind the presenter changed to a white-and-red flag and my insides turned weightless. *"Martial law continues in Poland,"* said the lady with her bleached teeth and wide-shouldered blazer.

"Despite the expulsion of foreign journalists, we have evidence that the Polish army has stationed tanks and thousands of troops in the

*five largest cities across the country in response to a wave of protests.
Experts say this move shows the government's desire to solve the crisis
without the help of the Kremlin, in an attempt to avoid an escalation
of violence. Despite this, the Soviets' military bases in Poland remain
on call."*

A photo filled the screen for a moment, showing a tank
parked on a snowy square, a couple of soldiers climbing out
of its hatch. Right behind them a building I recognized with a
pang of nostalgia—the Moskwa, a cinema where Karolina and
I used to go sometimes. But most remarkable: the poster that
hung above the tank, *"Apocalypse Now"* in bloody red type, the
new film by Coppola. For a moment the absurdity of it filled my
throat, threatened to suffocate me. All these years they'd let us
watch foreign films, allowing us glimpses of the world across
the Wall, of freedoms we didn't have. Did they really think we'd
be still forever?

I thought of the photographer and his courage, imagining
how the photo had made it out of the country: a roll of film
smuggled into West Germany, in a secret compartment or an
emptied tube of toothpaste. Anonymous figures trapped on
the wrong side of history, compressed and rolled up inside a
stranger's pocket. No matter what happens in the world, however brutal or dystopian a thing, not all is lost if there are people out there risking themselves to document it.

Little sparks cause fires too.

———

The morning after I saw you with Hania, I awoke feeling hung-
over. I remembered the night before and my body burned, like

a muscle sore all over. I lay in my bed, the sky gray and thin beyond the roofs of the blocks. My thoughts were like swallows, nosediving, avoiding the ground, flying up and away. I did not know how to stop them.

I got up to go to the bathroom but found *Pani* Kolecka in the living room sleeping. Something caught my eye, something small and dark. I approached her without making a sound. Blots covered the white duvet near her mouth. The same blots on a handkerchief she was holding in her hand: dark and irreversibly crimson. I had to stop myself from gasping out loud. She was breathing quietly, her white hair untied, spread out on her pillow like a halo. She looked like an ancient child. Fear rang, vibrated, like a church bell inside me. I pulled on my shoes and coat and hurried out into the cool morning. The nearest doctor's office was at the junction of Freedom and Lenin. I reached it, out of breath, just as they were opening. Already there was a group of people waiting by the door. A burly woman sat at the desk, looking at her schedule through thick glasses in which her eyes seemed tiny and miles away. When it was finally my turn, I told her about *Pani* Kolecka, my words stumbling over one another, the coughing, the blood.

"*Pan Doktor* is busy," she said, without looking up at me. "Earliest appointment is next week."

I insisted it was an emergency. She looked up at me for a moment, her phlegmatic face almost compassionate.

"In that case try the hospital. But I doubt she'll get in ahead of people with cut-off limbs and bleeding faces." Then she bent over her papers again.

"There must be something else you can do." I felt the moment slipping through my fingers. "Please, can't you make an exception?"

She raised her eyes toward me again, this time without a trace of empathy. "I told you what to do. Now stop blocking the line for your fellow citizens."

I stood in the cold morning, on the large Freedom Avenue, the sun far away, not warming, only blinding, throwing its wide light across the pavement onto the throngs of people hurrying to work with downcast faces.

One day, not long after Beniek's departure, I'd come home from school and found Granny crying on the couch. She was sobbing so hard she couldn't even tell me what was wrong, until she finally calmed down, saying that they'd found something in Mother's lungs. "It's not serious," she'd said, her tears beginning to dry on her cheeks. "The doctors will take care of it."

I stood in the cold morning and thought of how we'd sat in the hospital waiting for them to release Mother. How the clock in the waiting room had kept on ticking, how I'd held on to Granny's hand like a life vest. Smoke around us, oozing from the cigarettes held by nervous hands, the air gray and heavy, impenetrable. And, finally, the doctor, tall and dry, with a rigid face, saying he had bad news.

I walked to the nearest hospital, as the lady had said. It was an anonymous block I'd rode past countless times without ever seeing it. By the entrance, a man with crutches and a single leg, wearing a ragged dressing gown, was smoking a cigarette. Inside, gray corridors filled with the sharp smell of disinfectant. I pulled a number by the reception desk and took a seat in the queue on one of the benches. Groups of people were waiting in miserable silence, pierced only by the wails of patients lying on makeshift beds in the corridor. Hospital time took over, solid and unfeeling like a glacier. A man across from me was reading the *People's Tribune*. From the front page Party Chairman

Gierek glared at me. He was shaking hands with someone off-frame, his face mousy and thin-lipped and so utterly smug. My hands turned into fists inside my coat.

"Number thirty-three!"

It was my turn. Behind the glass, in her little cubicle, the nurse kept her eyes on the papers in front of her. I explained everything again, this time in more detail, trying to sound humble, to make it seem as serious as it felt.

"Is the patient here?" she interrupted, looking up for the first time.

"She's at home. I need to speak to a doctor, about the symptoms."

Her expression was lifeless, bored. "This is a hospital. Come back with the patient or take her to a doctor's office. Number thirty-four!" Her eyes discarded me.

"*Please,* I already went there, they have no appointments this week. Can't I just see a doctor for a moment?"

"I don't make the rules around here. Number thirty-four!"

I was about to protest again when someone shoved me away from the counter. Heat sprung up in me.

"Move," huffed the middle-aged man who'd been queuing behind me, smelling of sweat and onions. "You're not the only one here with problems."

I wanted to push him to the floor, to bang my fists against the lady's window, to scream my lungs out at them. I had a vision of myself doing just that, clear and vivid as if it were actually happening, and that scared me. I left without saying a word, without looking at her or the man again. I walked out onto the street, full of anger, feeling my legs tense. I walked as in a trance, hardly knowing where I was, until I felt a touch on my shoulders and I saw that I was on the New World Promenade, without knowing why. A stranger, a man in a suit and tie, was standing in front of me. Then I saw that it was you. You, looking like a different person. Your hair combed to the side, your leather shoes gleaming. I despised the sympathy I saw on your face.

"What are you doing here? What happened?" you asked as we stood in the middle of the street.

"*Pani* Kolecka . . . blood . . . no doctors." I felt tears rising in me. Tears of anger, I think. You put your hand on my shoulder, heavy and warm.

"Come on, Ludzio, we'll go and have coffee somewhere. I'm on my lunch break. We'll figure something out."

Your hand moved down to my back, guiding me along with you. I resisted its push.

"Let go of me, Janusz," I said through gritted teeth. "I've had enough of figuring things out. Enough of the talk."

You were undeterred; your hand stayed where it was.

"Ludzio, you need to calm down. Let's not make a scene in public. Let's go."

I pushed your hand off, its weight freeing me. "Go back to your office," I said, the fury pouring out of me. "And to her, if you like." Your face changed—understood, maybe. I turned quickly and left you standing there by yourself.

At the next empty telephone box, I dialed the only number I knew by heart. It rang several times, the beeping slow and plaintive.

"Ludwik, my child." The tenderness in her raspy voice shook me to the core. There was loneliness in that voice too, and exhaustion, a voice no longer used to speaking, one that had used up most of its words. "Is everything all right, my love?" she asked. I could sense the stillness of our old flat while around me throngs of people rushed past. I nodded into the receiver.

"Yes, Granny. I'm all right. I just wanted to hear you." I breathed in deeply. "It's so good to hear you. How are you?"

"I'm well," she said gravely. "Don't worry about me. May God protect you, my love. Come home soon, yes?"

Familiar guilt stirred in me, together with a longing for that faraway part of my childhood when everything had seemed almost carefree. "Yes, Granny, I will."

I put down the phone and walked on, agitated by my powerlessness. I walked with rage in my body, the old shame stirring, reawakening in the depths of my stomach, heavy and hard and sharp. I walked in the direction of the flat, my eyes fixed on the pavement, on the cracks in the concrete.

I came upon a large queue by a grocery store, and without knowing why, I stopped dead in my tracks. A rush went through the street, an undeniable shift of energy. As if it was about to thunder. Everyone, including the people in the queue, looked up. A cloud was falling from the sky, white and brilliant in the sunlight, sheets of paper, like wings, light and beautiful, like time, fluttering through the October air. It felt like a dream. Everyone stood still, women with their shopping nets and couples and children, stretching out their hands, looking up and around, letting the paper rain onto them. One of the sheets landed right by my feet. There was a red hand on it, seemingly dripping with blood and grabbing stalks of wheat. "Our Land, Our Food. OUT with the Soviets, IN with Our Rights!" it said in black letters. "Brothers and Sisters, Rise Up Tonight."

The words resonated in me like a voice speaking in my head. The crowd's amazement turned into apprehension as soon as they read the words. A child bent down to pick up the sheets, and his mother ripped them out of his hands, slapped him, and tore him away. Some hurried along; others looked up to the windows of the block that towered above us. I stood and watched, my senses in vertigo, my brain peculiarly calm. Already police sirens were howling and the crowd ran toward the blocks, the queue dispersed, people hurrying off like guilty foxes. In the confusion of it all, I bent down and picked up the leaflets, stuffing handfuls into my bag, wads of them, hearing my pulse pound in my ears. With the sirens coming closer, I jumped onto an approaching tram with my heart threatening to leap out of my chest.

Pani Kolecka was in the kitchen when I rushed in. She was leaning against the counter like a small, brittle tree in a dressing gown, caught by a fit of coughing. I helped her back to bed, her weight on me.

"How are you feeling?" I asked.

She looked at me with her small, watery eyes. "Maybe a little better, dear."

I helped her lie down. There was a large water stain where the blood had been on her sheet. I pretended not to see it.

In my room I took out my radio and turned it on. To cover her coughing. To cover my thoughts. I wanted to drown out the voices in my head that said that even having these flyers was a folly and could get me locked up. I didn't even hear the music. I sat on the edge of my bed with my head in my hands and my eyes closed.

I remembered the procession, moving slowly against the merciless wind under a sky the color of concrete, starting from the church, where Granny and I thanked everyone who'd come to pay their last respects. Consoling faces pressed against our frozen cheeks. Relief that Father hadn't shown up. Anger that Father hadn't shown up. The procession of regret and helplessness moved from the church along the streets of my childhood, the pavements of our games, past our flat and the park full of drunkards. A coffin carried to the cemetery, lowered into a hole. Earth hitting wood. Handful after handful, marking the end of our previous lives. Only Granny and I remained, life having skipped a generation. The flat seemed empty. Gone were the nights by the radio. The news no longer mattered. We no longer cared about outside. We turned inward. Granny started to attend church every day, getting up at five for the first mass. She resigned herself entirely to God, handing herself over to heaven like a premature donation. And me, I withdrew into my books. The radio in Mother's room remained covered forever. Not even music came out of it again. Not for many years.

I heard *Pani* Kolecka's coughing, sharp and thorny. Then I turned to the radio, lowered the volume, and moved the indicator to 101.2, the frequency still etched in my mind after all those years. I lay on my bed, the speakers to my ear, holding my breath. At first it was only music, but already I was calmed. I felt like that music, just for its origin, was cleansing me. And then, not long after, the familiar voice—deep and comforting and clear. There had been several of them who'd read the news over the years, and this was one of them. He was still there. It brought me back to the first time we'd all sat together, the three of us, around the radio in Mother's room. A voice that could not be spoken over, that would be listened to until the very end: "*Radio Free Europe. News at four o'clock. Friday, the tenth of October 1980.*"

He talked about the strikes that had gripped the country, halting production in dozens of known locations, including factories, mines, and shipyards. Workers had laid down their tools, demanding the revocation of the increase in meat prices, as well as better working conditions, the protection of the right to free speech, and the ability to form independent trade unions. There had been no violent clashes with the authorities so far. The strikes had not yet reached the capital. But insider sources indicated that they would, most likely that very afternoon. *"Residents are asked to remain indoors in case of any violent clashes with the authorities."*

I thought of Mother, of her pointless life, her passivity. Of the years she'd spent listening to the radio, explaining her truths to me, and all of it for what? She'd died a submissive employee at the Electricity Office and had never dared to speak up or live out any of her ideas.

"Your mother died out of loneliness," Granny would always repeat, claiming it was because she had never remarried after my father. But I think it was despair that killed her. Having done only things she didn't believe in, she must have been dead inside for years before her body finally gave up too.

I switched off the radio and got up, took my bag. I told *Pani* Kolecka I was going out for a walk.

She nodded weakly and whispered, "Look after yourself."

Outside, the air was pregnant with strife. The wind shook the trees, dry leaves rustled and dropped. I thought about where the demonstrations might be. The ones involving workers had always ended—violently or not—on the small square in front of the Party headquarters, by the National Museum.

I jumped onto a tram that went that way and felt my heart so clearly, so distinctly, that it might as well have been the engine pushing the tram along. The first people were returning from work, and the streets were full. Before the tram reached the crossing near the museum, it stopped abruptly, a sudden, violent jolt. People screamed, trying not to lose their footing. I held on hard in order not to fall. A small girl and a man were thrown to the floor, falling with their arms spread out. The man's walking stick slid to the end of the carriage. I helped him up, feeling his bones through the rough tweed of his jacket, his body light like a skeleton. He thanked me breathlessly. As we looked up, we saw the tram driver's booth empty, the driver outside talking to a policeman. There was a barricade in the middle of the street, a sturdy metal fence blocking passage.

"Everyone out!" the driver shouted as he came back. "The journey ends here."

The passengers looked at one another, confused.

"But why?" The little girl who'd fallen began to cry.

"Don't ask so many questions," her mother said. "Let's go."

We climbed out. On the other side of the barrier the street was empty, a field of concrete without any cars, only masses of people, ushered along the pavements by police. "Keep on walking. Keep on walking!" they shouted. "Hurry up! Go home, everyone, now!"

The crowd moved slowly, in silent obedience, only whispers here and there. We saw the emptiness of the street before us, the square in front of the Party building deserted, the building itself looming ominously above.

I felt the flow of the crowd carry me away from this scene and knew I had to find some way to stay where the action would be. This is when I saw a lady leave a building nearby, the door still ajar behind her. I ran and caught the door before it shut. I slipped inside and closed it behind me.

The staircase was silent. Doors led off it, with little signs indicating which offices they were. I walked up the stairs, carefully, slowly, aware of every step. From the first floor I could see the street and the crowds. I walked farther up. On the second floor one of the doors was half-open. I saw the inside of an office, two figures at the window, looking down onto the street. "Don't go out now, *Pani* Waleszka," said a man in a firm but friendly voice. "The demonstrators might come at any minute. You'd better stay here until they pass."

I slipped by them quickly, moving up to the third and last floor. It was all quiet. I saw the abandoned empty tram, the crowds on the pavements, the policemen pushing them along like cattle. The rest of the street was a wide and empty expanse, all the way to the headquarters. Policemen in helmets lined the barriers. I crouched, like a child in a tree house, hands on the cold windowsill, my fingers pulsing. The sun was beginning to set.

And then something approached. A murmur could be heard from far away, like the sound of a beehive, and a horde appeared on the horizon. I could not see them well at first, but as they came closer, I saw they were workers. They wore heavy boots and dark overalls and marched with banners held above their heads. They were chanting too. As soon as they appeared in the middle of the square, a rush went through the street, and everything changed, like rain falling after hours of pregnant, hovering clouds. The crowds on the pavements seemed to stop, to watch the marchers, and the police officers shouted louder, telling the people to move on. At the same time, a formation of policemen in helmets and masks marched in the direction of the strikers. A scream went through the bystanders—a policeman had hit someone with his stick. Without knowing why, I knew this was the moment. I got up. My heart was racing like a steam engine. I opened my bag, opened the window, felt the cool air against my face, the amplified buzz of the street in my ears. Then I turned my bag upside down above the street. The leaflets fluttered in the wind and glided up and away, like a scattered flock of doves. It was like the cloud I had seen earlier that day, the cloud that had given birth to this cloud, and this one too managed to stop time. I saw the faces in the street looking up, men and women and children, the police as well, confusion and amazement drawn on them as the paper rained down like giant confetti. I thought I heard banging against the front door three stories down. My heart pounded like a fist. I looked around. There were two doors. I tried both of them. They were locked. I knocked, urgently. Nothing happened. The banging on the front door became real and grew harder and louder. I ran down a flight. I tried one of the doors, without success. A crash shook the building, the sound of breaking wood. They'd broken through. Gushes of adrenaline flooded me. I weighed nothing. My insides were made of fire. I rattled on the door handles, desperate, gutted.

"Police!" angry voices shouted from downstairs, though I saw no one yet.

"Psst!"

I turned around. Behind me a door had opened and a man was looking at me intently, sizing me up. Then he gestured me in.

Heavy footsteps on the stairs. "Police!"

I jumped inside toward the man, and the door closed behind me.

There was heavy trampling of police boots just outside the door, shouting, running up to the top of the building, banging on the doors upstairs. I guessed they hadn't seen me. The man who had opened the door had an intelligent, tired face and graying hair that made him look older than he probably was. We exchanged quick looks. There was also a woman, younger than him, not so far from my age, I guessed, tall and broad, with a kind face. We heard the policemen coming back down the stairs, banging on the doors of this floor. Our door. The man and woman looked at each other, and he nodded in the direction of a corridor.

"Quick, *Pani* Waleszka, the kitchen."

The woman took me by the arm, and we hurried along the narrow corridor to a tiny kitchen with a view of the street. Before I could see anything going on outside, we heard more banging on the door. Then the sound of it being opened.

"Citizen," we heard a voice boom in the other room, "a suspect is hiding in this building. Have you seen him? A young man with light hair and a brown rucksack?"

"There is no one here apart from myself and my secretary," said the man calmly.

"Then you will let us search the space."

Their boots crossed the threshold.

The woman and I looked at each other in the tiny kitchen. Right behind the door was another, very narrow door, painted the same color as the wall. *Pani* Waleszka opened it quickly, took out some brooms that were inside, and pushed me in. I fit sideways, and she closed the door. I heard her shoving the brooms up against it, and running in other parts of the office, and the sound of her heels on the wooden floor of the corridor.

"Is there anyone in that other room, citizen?"

"No, Officer," said her voice, betraying no tension.

The kitchen door was flung open, and the door to my hiding place trembled. I could see them through a crack, a tiny slice of them. I thought my heart would burst. There were two. Flushed, angry men in uniforms, inches away. I would never see you again. Panic gripped me and pulled me into an abyss. The policemen moved quickly, looking around the kitchen and out onto the street through the window.

"Shit," one of them whispered, banging his fist on the kitchen counter.

"All clear!" shouted the other one into the corridor.

There was a scratching on the door.

"You can come out now," said the woman's voice. I don't know how long I had been in there, listening to the sound of the policemen thundering through the building, banging on doors, searching the flats and offices, returning to interrogate the man and the woman and to take down their details, and the commotion outside, the screams of the crowds, and then, gradually, the dying down of any sound except for the wailing of sirens. Finally I'd heard cars honking, and the buzzing of the trams, and then this scratching.

The door to my cell opened. They both stood there, a light bulb hanging above their heads, night in the street behind them. I forced my body out of its hiding place, dusted myself off, aware of their eyes on me. They had their coats on, and both wore a look of exhaustion and curiosity.

"That was very brave of you," said *Pani* Waleszka.

"And foolish," said the man, with a hint of a smile in his gray eyes.

"I know," I said, feeling embarrassed. "Thank you. You saved me."

Pani Waleszka poured a glass of water and handed it to me.

"Yes, that was rather close," said the man, eyeing me. "And an interesting spectacle too, those flying papers. What an idea, to throw propaganda out there when the whole of the city's police is mobilized in the street. If it hadn't been for us, you would have spent tonight in prison." He smiled, stretching out his hand. "I'm Tadeusz Rogalski, attorney," he said. His hand was large and soft, his fingers like little pincushions.

"I'm Ludwik."

"And this is *Pani* Waleszka, my secretary." We shook hands.

"Call me Małgosia," she said.

"So what happened?" I asked.

They looked at each other. "They dispersed the strikers," said Małgosia hesitantly, unwillingly almost. "A few people got hurt."

"Did anyone die?"

"We don't know," said the man, looking at the floor. "Ambulances came and took people away."

"Do you think it's safe for me to go out there?"

"They might still be looking for you," he said. "Or not. But we'd better not take any risks. We'll take the back entrance. Let's go."

We went down the dark stairs very quietly. Before we reached the ground floor I could hear the noise of passing cars—the entrance door was unhinged, leaning against a wall. We slipped into a long, dark corridor that led in the opposite direction, where *Pan* Tadeusz quickly unlocked a door. We crept into an unlit courtyard. There was light in a couple of the windows that faced us, the lamps behind the drawn curtains somehow ominous, like secrets about to be unveiled. We hurried toward a white Trabant, and they made me lie on the back seat. The car started, the engine vibrating, my cheek cool against the leather. Driving out of the courtyard, we flowed into the arteries of the city, inserting ourselves into its body like an unsuspected virus. From below, I watched the houses and monuments rush past, both familiar and new from that perspective. Police sirens howled in the distance, and then the Trabant stopped at the mouth of the *blokowisko*.

"Good night, Ludwik," the man said, turning around to me. "Watch out for yourself. And don't push your luck."

CHAPTER 5

THIS MORNING, LIKE EVERY morning, I took the subway across to Manhattan. I sat at my desk and tried to work, but my mind was back home. I had a bad feeling. Some sort of intuition. As soon as midday struck, I left the office and walked a couple of blocks over to the telephone box on the corner of Third and East Forty-Third. No one is ever at that corner, and no one was there today. I called Jarek. He's a fixer, a connector, knowing everything about everyone in the community. He works late shifts at a factory down in Queens, and I knew he'd be home.

"Did you hear?" he said with his smoker's voice, almost immediately after picking up the phone. "The ZOMO killed nine miners in Katowice. They were protesting the martial law. Can you believe it? First they lock our people in our country, then they jail them, now they shoot them in the street. Sons of bitches. This time they're gonna pay for it."

A shiver ran down my back and across my lips. "Are you sure?"

He spat out his words like bullets. "Sure as fuck. This is serious."

I thought of the miners, and it struck me that they could have been the same people I had seen a year earlier from that window where I threw the flyers. Or it could have been me.

But then, I had been a coward compared to them. I had hidden under window ledges, in kitchen closets; I had not been in the streets demanding my right to be heard. Now I was an ocean away, wearing a new suit. I wondered about your role in all this, what kind of pact you'd made with yourself. Because we all make one, even the best of us. And it's rarely immaculate. No matter how hard we try.

"Głowacki? Are you still there?" Jarek's voice brought me back. "You all right? Got family in Katowice?"

"No," I said. "I'm OK." I thanked him, which felt macabre, and cut the call. Then, for the umpteenth time that week, I dialed Granny's number.

The tone went *"Beepbeepbeepbeepbeep,"* repeating mercilessly like a reproach.

I walked back to work, waited for the sadness to pass.

———

The night after the flyers I slept deeply, dreamlessly, as if floating underwater. I was unmoored, a ship that had finally left its harbor, only to be pushed by the wind without any control of its own. When I awoke, I hardly knew who or where I was. It felt as if I'd returned from a long journey underneath the sea. I was on my bed, fully dressed; my bag lay beside me on the floor. Outside, the sun stood high in a spotless sky.

I heard *Pani* Kolecka coughing. I got up to check on her, the remains of sleep diffused by anxiety. There was no blood on her or on the sheets. I went to the kitchen and prepared her tea, wondering what I'd make her to eat, wondering whether I'd try the doctor's office again. Wondering whether it was even safe for me to go out onto the street. Whether the police wouldn't somehow come looking for me, or whether I was being paranoid. And then, as I served *Pani* Kolecka the tea, the doorbell rang. The ringing was shrill like a cry.

Pani Kolecka looked at me. We never had anyone over, except for a neighbor who came every Friday to knit with *Pani* Kolecka. But it wasn't Friday.

"*Pan* Ludwik, are you expecting visitors?"

I shook my head, listening for movement.

The doorbell rang again, with more urgency.

"Won't you see who it is?" she asked.

I walked down the corridor toward the door, my knees weak. I closed my eyes. My heart was beating hard, reminding me of the previous night's narrow escape, of the small closet, the policemen standing inches away from me. I made myself open my eyes, look through the peephole. In the globular glass your face was large and round like a moon, your body tiny underneath it, attached to you like a stalk to a flower. I felt relief rush through me. I opened the door. We looked at each other for a long moment, without saying anything.

"I brought you something." You pointed at the shopping net in your hand. I beckoned you inside. In the corridor you took off your shoes. It struck me how strange it was to have you there, how small you made the place look. I introduced you to *Pani* Kolecka. Her face lit up in a way I hadn't seen in weeks.

"So you're the nice *pan* who Ludwik went traveling with this summer?"

You nodded, the perfect son-in-law.

"Would you like some tea?" she asked, looking at you in adoration, when a fit of coughing took hold of her.

"No, thank you," you said, waiting for her to stop. "I won't trouble you for long. Ludwik told me you haven't been well. I managed to get you a doctor's appointment. Tomorrow at ten." You handed her a card.

She looked at it, squinting, reaching for her glasses. "But, *Pan* Janusz, this is a *private* doctor," she muttered, looking concerned. "I don't think I can—"

"He won't accept payment," you said. "Don't worry."

She considered you for a moment, very seriously. "*Pan* Janusz, how can I accept this?"

"It's nothing. A favor being returned, that's all." You glanced at me for a moment.

Pani Kolecka's face broke into an involuntary smile. "I don't know how to thank you. Please, stay for lunch."

"Thank you, but I have to go, and you need to rest. Another time. When you feel better." You got up and shook her hand and came through to the corridor with me.

I wanted to thank you, but I couldn't.

"I was worried about you," you said. "You seemed so upset yesterday. I waited for you at the pool last night. And with the demonstrations escalating . . . Did you hear?"

"I'm fine," I said, managing to keep a steady face, watching yours relax.

You pulled out a packet from the net bag and handed it to me. It was large and heavy. "Chicken," you said. "So you can make her broth."

You knelt down to slip your shoes back on.

"How did you get all this?"

You straightened up, your face right in front of mine. "I told you, there are ways."

"*How?*"

"A contact. I'll explain soon. Take care of *Pani* Kolecka. And come to see me when you can." You kissed me quickly, for no one to see or hear, and slipped out, your footsteps echoing in the stairwell.

I took *Pani* Kolecka to the doctor. I'd pushed all the clothes I'd worn that night of the flyers far under my bed, and for the outing I put on a green hat *Pani* Kolecka had knitted. We arrived at the doctor's, a small, quiet practice in the south of the city. *Pani* Kolecka was silent with awe as we sat on the leather couches of the empty waiting room, while I flicked through the latest copy of the *People's Tribune,* dreading to see a phantom drawing of me in there. But there was not even a mention of the strikes. Nothing. As if that night had never happened.

The doctor examined *Pani* Kolecka with unusual care and gave her a dose of French antibiotics that he took from a glass cabinet behind his desk. On the way home, we passed a line of policemen. I held my breath, but they didn't even look at me.

That week I didn't leave the flat. My mind had a storm raging inside it, and outside the autumn rains began. It rained for days on end. The drops drummed onto the roofs and hammered the streets. Thunder growled like the anger of our forefathers. It felt like the city was under attack, like the city and its streets might start to give way, dissolve, its life flowing into the Wisła and out into the cold depths of the sea.

I sat by the window and watched. I couldn't bring myself to listen to the secret frequency again. A great weariness overcame me every time I thought of it, and of that night, and of the abyss of fear that had opened up as I'd stood in that closet. Something inside me had shut down. The radio remained silent.

Instead I took care of *Pani* Kolecka, watched her get better little by little with the medicine the doctor had given her. A weight lifted from my soul. She was weak still, but the fits grew shorter and fainter. I'd make her tea and sit by her side and listen. She told me about the journeys she'd made with her husband, the work trips they'd gone on abroad, to Tunisia and Algeria. She showed me her photos, of dry, desert-like landscapes with palm trees and orange-brown earth and low square houses made by hand. There she was, a younger version of herself in an ankle-length dress with flowers and a straw hat, looking proudly into the camera. Next to her, her husband, tall and stocky, his square face content, a big white hat on his head. Everything had been different there, she said, smiling to herself. She told me how they used their right hand to eat and their left to clean themselves.

"Those Arabs are very different to us. But so kind." There were photos of them, tall, dark men in white robes and sandals and beautiful beards. She showed me the rocks they'd brought back, the basalt and the crystals, the granite and shimmering minerals. She held them before me like the greatest treasures on earth and talked of her late husband and how much she missed him, and her small eyes shone like those precious stones.

"You need to hold on to what you have," she murmured, more to herself than to me, her veiny hands clasped around a cup of tea. "You never know when you'll lose what you hold dearest."

I nodded, pulling her in for a hug. She smelled like home, of mothballs and comfort. I thought of you.

Finally, the rains stopped. The world had been washed, and the city was still standing. Soon after, I received a note from Professor Mielewicz, asking me to come to his office the following week. I went into the bathroom with the big pair of scissors from the kitchen and began to cut my hair. Strands floated into the sink and onto the floor, lightly, like feathers, like the flocks of leaflets released by my hands. My head felt lighter. I looked at my face, smiled at myself, cut everything even. I looked good, I thought, shorn and new. Outside, the air already smelled different. Fresher, sharper—summer was gone. The autumn wind caressed my head, made it feel like new skin. The ladies walking their dogs down in the courtyards had changed into coats, wore them unbuttoned as they gossiped with one another, leashes tied around their soft, wrinkled wrists. Puddles filled the holes in the streets. The flowers and berries had disappeared from the market stalls, replaced by mushrooms.

I boarded the tram, rattled along with it, saw the banks of Praga colored in a riot of dark greens and reds. I got to your street, to your house, ran up the stairs to your door. You opened up and we held each other, my face in your neck and your warm breath in my ear like gentle whispering. Your hand caressing my new hair.

"Is she feeling better?" you asked in a whisper.

I nodded, holding on to you tighter. "Thank you," I said into your neck. I could feel you smiling against my cheek. I had meant to ask you again how you'd managed it, the doctor, the chicken; I'd planned the questions before coming—about Hania too, especially about her. But I couldn't bring myself to ask. I was too happy to see you, too relieved. Too weary to struggle. I let myself fall on the bed. The cold air gave us goose bumps as we undressed. We found warmth beneath your covers. We tested our strengths, wrestled with the urgency of desire, conjured up heat. Our bodies like firestones. You had me, and I had you. But it didn't feel like the other times, the first times. It felt like we were settling a score, evening something out. Like we needed this, this language, this code, to know where we were, and who. And that we were both still holding on.

Afterward you got up and switched on the radio, sitting on your haunches, turning the tune button. Your arched back defined, your ass resting on your heels. Your tan had faded, I realized, and so had mine. Finally you found a station, a piano concerto, maybe Mozart. You lit a cigarette and came back to bed, the smoke gently floating, caressing the air. I felt weightless, again like one of the leaflets I had released into the air. I closed my eyes.

"Maybe you were right," I said, feeling you lie down next to me.

"About what?" You blew out your smoke. It mingled with the air above us.

"About needing to stay calm and finding other ways. I was foolish."

It felt good to say this, to shed conscience like a coat. If only the lightness would last, like another toke, another exhalation. The piano played joyfully, relentlessly. My eyes remained closed.

"You were scared," you whispered. "But now you know that there's no need for that." Your mouth covered mine. The smoke flowed from you to me, down into my lungs, filling me up, making me feel, for one moment, like I would burst.

That Saturday you and I met by the Łazienki Gardens. It was my favorite park in the city and the only place I remember visiting the one time I'd come to Warszawa as a child with Mother and Granny. We'd taken a boat on the lake, fed the swans and the squirrels, had seen the other, complete families—mothers, fathers, and children. We'd visited the white palace on the island of the lake, the same palace that had been part of the king's pleasure gardens and now served as a distraction for good workers and their families. As we were leaving, climbing up a gentle slope, we'd seen a man stacking blocks of hay under a small thatched roof. "Who is this for?" Mother had asked him. She was so elegant that day; I remember the moss-green hat she wore, the matching gloves. "The deer," he'd said, and continued working. That had seemed incredible to me, that deer should live in the park, hidden from everyone's sight.

That Saturday night, when it was already dark and the gates of the gardens were locked, I imagined them, the deer, racing unhindered through the grounds, across the untended meadows, up and down the hills, along the tree-lined paths, their hooves clattering on the gravel and stirring the sleeping swans. What freedom to live like that, protected and boundless at once.

You were waiting for me in the light of a streetlamp. You wore a brown corduroy jacket, and your hair was combed to the side, like that time you'd stopped me in the street in your suit, the day of the flyers. Like that day, you looked like a different person, and this both scared and excited me.

"Very chic," I said, clicking my tongue, hiding my discomfort.

You smiled. "You look great too."

I'd worn my only jacket, a white shirt, and my good shoes. "Are you sure it's not strange for me to go to her party?"

You laughed briefly and placed your hand on the back of my neck. "There'll be lots of people there. You'll blend right in."

We walked the avenue along the park, past the tall government buildings patrolled by soldiers in berets. Only some windows were illuminated, the rest dark and dormant. You led us into a side street, lined by prewar buildings with large balconies on each floor. In front of us a woman in a fur coat and high heels was walking a sausage dog, her coat as shiny as her pet, a cigarette burning lazily in her gloved fingers. We stopped by a large entrance gate.

You pressed a button on the *domofon,* and a crackling man's voice came from the grid, asking who it was. You said your name. There was a buzzing noise, and you pushed the massive door open with the weight of your whole body.

I had never been to a house like this. It was a splendid *kamienica,* an apartment building from before the war, one of the few that had survived. The entrance hall was high and vaulted, the ceiling covered in stucco flowers. A carpet led toward another set of doors, revealing a staircase, old and curved, with iron railings. You called the lift. We got in and rose weightlessly in the little silent box. In the glow of the single light bulb we inspected ourselves in the mirror. We looked serious and strangely put together, more grown-up than I'd ever seen us. The lift came to a halt and we got out, and you rang the bell by a wide double door. Subdued music and chatter emanated from behind it. Footsteps approached, the door opened, and a hulking figure appeared.

"Janusz!" He opened his arms wide and you embraced, kissing each other on the cheek. It took me a moment to realize it was the friend I'd seen you with at camp, Maksio Karowski. He wore a velvet jacket and a shirt with a big collar and had the same confident and indifferent way about him that had struck me before. We shook hands, his almost crushing mine.

"Nice to meet you," he said, his hand strong and warm, something about his momentary attention making me feel strangely charmed.

We followed him through a wood-paneled corridor into a large room filled with smoke and people. Music blasted throughout the place, hot and loud, rockingly hypnotic. Couples danced in the middle of the room or lay spread out on a white yeti carpet. The only light came from lamps on the floor, one by a large television, another behind a pair of giant palm trees in pots. Maksio led us to the end of the room, where grand bay windows looked out onto the dark and seemingly infinite treetops of the park.

"Help yourself," he said, pointing to a table covered in bottles and plates. "I need to check on somebody." He winked at us and disappeared in the crowd.

There were vodkas and whiskies and gins and vermouths and bottles I had never seen before and colorful plates of aspic meats and pineapple rings and cheese cubes. I wanted to taste everything. I ate some grapes and downed some whisky, feeling the liquid's journey through my body, earthy and sweet and unburdening. The music and the laughter of the people all merged in my mind, spinning me into its net. I didn't recognize anyone in the dim light of the room; every silhouette seemed equally important and glamorous: girls in dresses and clogs and hair piled high, boys in high-waisted blue jeans and tight shirts and jackets.

"This place is out of this world!" I cried into your ear, over the sound of the music, and you nodded, and your mouth formed the words *I know.*

We had another drink and had just started to move to the music when an arm snaked itself around my waist from behind, orange fingernails and dangling bracelets.

"I almost didn't recognize you with that hair, handsome," said a mouth by my ear.

It was Karolina. Lips the color of pomegranates, lashes large and thick and heavy with mascara like clotted spider legs.

"What are you doing here?" I pressed her against me, relieved to see a familiar face.

"I was invited, I swear!" she cried, taking my head in between her hands, kissing me on the mouth. I could feel her lipstick rubbing off, the petrol smell of her breath.

She laughed and held her outstretched hand toward you like a lady. "I don't think we've ever properly met."

You kissed the hand obligingly, playing her game.

I took her by the waist. "Are you drunk?"

"As a sailor. It would be stupid not to be." She raised her glass, swayed on her heels.

And then the music stopped. The record had come to an end; the low crackle of the speakers could be heard between the suddenly naked chatter of the crowd. We looked at each other, bemused, in anticipation. A new record was placed on the deck by a gangly boy in green bell-bottoms. At once a string of quick, light beats prepared the room, gathered our attention, ecstatic, simple, and single-minded. And before we knew it, Blondie's siren voice had filled the room, sending a rush through us. We didn't know the words, not a single one, but we understood everything about "Heart of Glass"—all its elation, its decadence, the pleasure of self-indulgence. We made our way through the crowd to the middle of the room, where we dissolved ourselves in her voice, in its high flight, in the rising and falling melody, in the motif of the beat, the beat that was there from beginning to end and begged to be followed. Our heads spun along with the record. Our bodies became instruments of the song, extensions of it, and we formed as one, dancing in a triangle, swaying from side to side as if possessed. When the song ended, another one began to play, one just as good and catchy and seductive, and we gave ourselves to it. It was as if someone had taken us all and placed us on a platform on top of the world. We danced until sweat ran down our backs and foreheads and we could no longer catch our breath.

Later, the three of us took a break, filled our glasses, smoked by the large windows looking out over the black expanse of the park. The windows had glazed over with our heat, and someone opened one, letting in the cool evening air. That's when I saw her. On the other side of the room, talking with a blond boy in a pair of dark sunglasses. She wore a long sequined dress, and her hair was large and frizzy, almost standing up from her head. She was an apparition. Then her eyes fell on you, and she made her way across the room.

"How lovely you could make it!" She threw herself around your neck as if that's what it was there for, her flowery-spicy perfume enveloping us all. Her eyeshadow was blue and sparkling like Ziggy Stardust's. Her eyes came to rest on me. "I was watching you earlier," she said, speaking slowly as if pronouncing a verdict. "*Fabulous* dancing. And that hair suits you." She glanced at Karolina. "This must be your girl?"

Karolina laughed with her mouth thrown open. "No, just a friend," she cried, looking over to me and straightening her face. "Just a friend."

Hania smiled politely, looking at you and then back at Karolina. "Well, maybe we can find you someone here—there are plenty of boys around. Janusz, shall we dance?"

You nodded and let her arm slide around yours.

"See you later," she cooed, and you were off.

Karolina and I poured ourselves another drink, on the brink of total drunkenness now, and fell onto a wide, soft couch in the corner, where we could see the whole room. The whisky was still good and strong; its warmth went straight from my stomach to my head.

"I'm so glad you're here, kiddo," Karolina said, her legs thrown over each other, almost lying on the couch.

"Me too," I slurred. "Who invited you, anyway?"

She laughed. "Excuse *you*. Maksio invited me." She pointed at him on the other side of the room, dancing closely with a blond girl in a miniskirt. "The sleaze."

I considered Karolina from the side, her profile clear against the white of the couch. She looked tired, and for the first time it occurred to me that we were all aging, that we would not be young forever.

"But how do you even know him?" I asked.

She shrugged, looking at the floor. "We may or may not have had a fling," she said quietly, with a guilty smile.

"*How?*"

"He came and sat next to me on the bus on our way back from camp." She shrugged. "He knows how to speak to girls."

"I thought he wasn't your type," I said, stunned.

"He isn't, but I was feeling lonely. Anyway—here's to all the fun we've had at his cost." We clinked glasses and took another deep comforting sip.

"But I thought it was Hania's party," I said.

"Goodness," Karolina said with a sigh, rolling her eyes, "doesn't he tell you anything? Maksio and Hania are siblings."

I was taken aback, without quite knowing why. "That makes sense, I suppose."

"Yes, it does," she said, looking at Maksio, who was now kissing the blonde. "The same sense of entitlement. Did you see how she dragged Janusz away from us?"

I shrugged, trying to keep my mind at bay. "They're friends. Why shouldn't she dance with him?"

A slow song was playing now, a dark, profound voice singing in English, lamenting something bygone. And the dancing couples turned and swayed in their own orbits, their own planetary paths. I couldn't see you on the crowded dance floor. I wished it could be us out there.

"So how are you?" asked Karolina, seeing me look for you.

I shrugged, feeling my head spin again. "Good, I guess. I'm seeing Mielewicz next week. I think he's read my proposal."

"And?"

"I don't know . . . He hasn't said anything yet. But I enjoyed writing it, more than I thought I would. I'd love to do it."

"What if it doesn't work out?" She looked worried for a moment, and I wondered how real this concern was and how much of it bitterness concealed. Bitterness about her own situation.

"Somehow I think it could turn out all right, you know?" I said.

"Wow, you've become awfully optimistic lately," she replied with only a trace of irony.

The dancing couples before us moved, parted to the sides like a curtain—revealing you. You and Hania. Entwined in your own secret constellation. Her eyes were closed, her cheek resting on your shoulder, your fingers wrapped around her gleaming sequined waist . . .

I couldn't think straight—my mind was like an erring line. But my body reacted all by itself, fossilizing my insides.

"Looks like they get on well," said Karolina, watching you darkly. You and Hania swayed to the waves of the song.

"I don't think she's his type." I held on tightly to the banister of my own words.

"Ludzio, with this house, you're everyone's type." She said this without taking her eyes off you and Hania. She said it almost absentmindedly. Then the other couples moved in their rotations and hid you from our sight again. And I looked back at Karolina. Her words remained in the air, heavy, unwilling to go away, like a fog.

"You're exaggerating," I said. "Since when are you such a bloody pragmatist?"

She laughed, as if to appease me. "Not me, Ludzio. But everyone else." The tip of her middle finger traced the brim of her glass. Then she looked around the room, low and mysterious with the dim light and the palm trees. Her eyes shimmered. "It's beautiful here. And there are no queues for Scotch whisky." She clinked her glass to mine and took another deep sip.

"You're drunk," I said, feeling the drink turn bitter in my mouth. The music played on. The couples danced carelessly. "I need the bathroom," I said, and stumbled off. Someone pointed me to a door at the end of the long corridor, and I slipped inside. My head was spinning. I went to the sink and splashed water over my face. The only light came from silver bulbs arranged around the wide mirror, like in a Hollywood boudoir. It made me look tired—somehow older, like Karolina had earlier. My eyes fell on a large square machine in the corner. I believe this was the first time I'd seen a washing machine with my own eyes. It glistened in the light of the room, solid and reassuring, its little round door like the entrance to a spacecraft. I thought of Granny, kneeling over a metal basin, pouring scalding water from a kettle, dipping each shirt, each sock, each handkerchief into the water, all her life, with a block of brown soap in her sore hands—rubbing, scouring, fingers burning.

When I returned to the dancing room, Karolina was gone. I sat on the couch next to a kissing couple, watched the people on the dance floor, and fell deeper and deeper into a sense of alienation. And just when I was wondering what I was doing there and had resolved to leave, the music stopped mid-song and the lights turned off. The crowd came to a baffled stand-still, and from the corridor a halo of light, and a set of deep voices began to sing: *"Sto lat, sto lat . . ."* I got up to see. You and Maksio appeared in the door with a cake so big you had to hold it between the two of you. A circle of candles burned in its cen-ter. Within an instant the whole room had joined in: *"Sto lat, sto lat,"* they sang. "A hundred years, a hundred years shall you live for us." Even I joined in, swept up by the momentum. The cake traveled slowly through the crowd toward Hania, who stood in the middle of the room, beaming with delight. You and Maksio reached her just as the song came to an end, a storm of cheers and congratulations raging through the air, boys whis-tling with fingers in their mouths. Hania bent over the cake. In the darkness of the room the candles were the only source of light. They lit her face from below. She took a large breath and blew out the little flames, her eyes half-closed, her painted face strained with effort. I told myself that she looked like a witch, but I hardly believed it. I couldn't bring myself to hate her. The applause was deafening. Hania kissed Maksio on the cheek and then threw her arms around your neck. Someone called out a toast, to which the whole room lifted their glasses. And then the low lights came back on and the music started up again. I sat down, finished my drink, and resolved to leave. That is when I saw you making your way toward me through the crowd with a piece of cake in each hand. You were smiling at me, and I couldn't bring myself to smile back. Sitting down next to me, you passed me a piece of cake.

"Are you all right? You look a little . . . something."

"I'm OK," I lied. The cake was a layered chocolate-and-cream affair, surprisingly heavy and wet. I could feel it through the flimsy, Bible-page-thin napkin.

"Have some," you said, biting into your piece. "It's good."

"I don't feel like it."

You wiped your mouth with the back of your hand and looked me over.

"What is it?"

For a moment I said nothing, determined to punish you through silence. But then the need to speak up became inevitable and the words came to me all at once, rising up and taking shape like a balloon.

"*She's* your contact, isn't she?" I said.

To my surprise your face remained relaxed, unconcerned.

You took another bite from the cake. "Is *that* your problem?" You said this with your mouth full. It disgusted me, and I realized then that your power over me went so unthinkingly far beyond the physical. You swallowed and looked at me. "Yes, she is. So?"

"So?" I looked you over, braced myself to continue, trying not to leave the path of confrontation I had chosen. "She's in love with you, Janusz. Clearly so. And you're leading her on."

"Keep your voice down, will you?" There was urgency in your

tone, and you put the half-finished piece of cake back onto the napkin with an irritated look. "Stop being so dramatic. Aren't we having fun? Just enjoy. Enjoy it, Ludwik."

"*Enjoy?*" I was stunned, confused, searched your face for an explanation that would give all this some meaning. "Do you think this is fun for me, watching you two dancing together like lovers?"

You surveyed the room with one quick look and leaned into me, your mouth by my ear.

"I told you I can take care of things for us. Don't you trust me?"

I moved away from you, from your words. "You think you're doing me a *favor* with this? I can do without that sort of help." I made to get up, but you held me back.

"Oh yeah? You'd rather let *Pani* Kolecka cough herself to death?" You looked at me challengingly then. "Everyone is leading someone on," you continued, your eyes narrowed. "Isn't that what you say? That the country is mismanaged, that everything is unfair? So what's wrong with taking things into your own hands and not letting yourself go under? Huh?"

My untouched piece of cake had soaked through the napkin, lying sticky and heavy in my hand. I looked at you, your previously familiar features, and it seemed as if your face had transformed before my eyes. There was a tightness around your eyes and lips that I had never seen before. Out on the dance floor, Hania swayed softly in the arms of the blond guy with the sunglasses. She looked serene. The boy's face was immobile, only his mouth opened to smile from time to time, revealing a set of perfect white teeth.

"There must be other ways," I said quietly.

You looked weary. "Oh yeah? Which ones? Tell me."

"I don't know. Going away, for example."

"You mean *running* away?" You looked at me imploringly. "Trust me. I am not promising her anything. I am not hurting her."

"Not yet," I said.

"I can handle it," you insisted. "There is no harm in this. And it needs to be done."

"*Why?* Tell me. There is nothing we need from them anymore. *Pani* Kolecka is healthy again. We're fine now."

Your face distorted, hardened again. "You still don't understand, do you? We will need something again soon enough. Life is full of these times. And how will we cope then?"

I tried to assemble my thoughts, to resist. But nothing came.

"You're the one who didn't see a future in our country," you said, your voice soothing. "*Here* it is."

I followed your eyes, taking in that splendid room. Among the people dancing I saw Karolina, with her arms around a boy I'd never seen before, a glowing cigarette drooped from her fingers.

"You'll get to know them," you went on, encouraged by my silence. "You'll see. I told Hania about your doctorate—she seemed impressed. We're having dinner on Wednesday night at Mozaika. She said you should come."

Again, I said nothing. The night was growing old, and behind the wide windows of the splendid room, darkness was giving way to another morning.

CHAPTER 6

THE WEDNESDAY AFTER THE party I went to see the professor. I was more nervous than I thought I'd be, my mind circling in hostile loops as I walked the New World Promenade. The air felt thin. I arrived at the office, knocked on the door. A subdued "Come in" resounded from inside. I affected a confident smile. The professor gave me a weary nod.

"Please sit down," he said, his voice strangely lifeless. His face seemed grayer than it had a couple of weeks earlier, as if he'd aged since the last time I saw him. The silence between us was heavy and seemed to sit entirely on my chest.

"The board liked your proposal, Głowacki," he finally said, in a strangely formal voice. I looked at him, uncertain. "They like it more than they want to admit, actually. Your writing is good, your ideas worth exploring. You know that."

I didn't know whether it was my turn to speak. A pained smile distorted his face.

"But, as you might imagine, there are other forces at play too."

My gut contracted. I looked at the professor, trying to read his face. I felt completely powerless.

"There are other candidates," he went on, sounding tired. "Their proposals aren't as good as yours. But . . ." He took off his glasses, rubbed his eyes. "Some of them have contacts."

Another silence, another glance from him to me, as if he wanted me to release him from this chore. My mind in free fall.

"The final decision hasn't been made yet, but if things continue as they are now, it doesn't look good for you. I need you to know this." He let out a sigh, looked at his desk, his papers, then back to me.

"Then why have you called me in? What do you want me to do?" My voice was small and angry, more than I wanted it to be.

The professor looked at me softly, as if he'd expected my anger.

"I know how disappointing this must be for you."

This made me feel more desperate.

He placed both of his hands on the papers before him and leaned across the desk toward me, so I could see the single gray hairs of his moustache and his kind, round face, closer than I'd ever seen it.

"I know you are not in the Party," he said, his voice barely more than a whisper, "and it's too late to join now anyway. Even if you wanted to." He lowered his eyes, maybe embarrassed by what he was about to propose. "But maybe you *know* someone, Ludwik? Someone you forgot to mention and who could help tip the balance in your favor?"

His gaze on me was suddenly like yours the night of the party, expectant, too much so. I sat still, entrenched in silence.

Finally, he nodded, visibly awkward. "Think about it. Maybe someone will come to mind. It would a pity for you to miss this opportunity."

It almost seemed that if I didn't acknowledge this moment, it wouldn't be true. I remained silent.

The professor stood, attempted a smile. "Let me know as soon as you can, will you?"

I managed to rise, to nod into space. We shook hands, mine limp, his far too big, and a moment later I was standing in the corridor with oblivious strangers hurrying past me in all directions. The academic year had started, and new students were walking the grounds. New faces so young-looking I could hardly believe they'd finished high school. They strode around as if the place was theirs, as if no other student had ever been there before them. I left the campus, staggered through the streets, felt the wind bite at my fingers and neck, gnawing at my head.

It was a cold day, maybe the first really cold day of the season, and I was unprepared. I had neither scarf nor gloves nor hat. I had underestimated the weather. The trees were losing their leaves. I erred about the streets, hardly knowing which way I was going. I just walked, put one foot in front of the other, feeling the vague protection of the movement, its rhythm lulling me. But not enough to make me forget that my allowance would run out in a matter of weeks. Suddenly I had no vision of the future, only a dreadful void. I'd been naive, stupid even. I saw it then. As long as I walked, though, I didn't have to think, didn't have to face anything for long.

When I came to my senses, I was on Marszałkowska Street, and there you stood, talking to a guy in a pair of sunglasses, the one Hania had danced with at the party. He introduced himself as Rafał and gave me his hand with a wry smile. It was unnerving not to see his eyes. We looked at each other, you and I, but we couldn't say anything.

The sun was already weak and descending; it grew colder, but I didn't feel it anymore. From where we stood, on the city's straightest, longest street, you could see all the way to Constitution Square, with its gigantic Stalinist buildings and carvings of muscled workers and strong, healthy mothers, and even farther, past the damaged Church of the Holiest Saviour and toward the tiny square beyond, where Hania and Maksio lived. It was only four o'clock, but night had already started to envelop us. We stood and waited under the neon sign of the restaurant—a large red "Mozaika" in handwritten style—like a beacon of something better and more modern that might brighten our lives. We talked to Rafał, but my mind was absent. I can't remember a word we exchanged. I can't remember anything until a black Vespa stopped right in front of us. Hania was wearing a biker jacket and high boots, her hair untied, and Maksio had on a thick Alpine-style sweater the color of cream. All their clothes looked new and foreign. I stared at them in awe, as if they were a pair of actors from a Fellini film. We kissed on the cheek and shook hands. They seemed genuinely glad to see me, and already the tingling warmth of flattery began to soothe my nerves.

We walked into Mozaika, where it was warm and soft. A low-ceilinged room decked out in red carpet and uniformed black-tie staff, and—again—those giant potted palm trees, each leaf big enough to wrap a baby inside, reaching into the room languidly and lazily and utterly aware of their own magnificence. The people there were the sort one never saw walking in the street, and so one would have been excused for thinking they didn't exist: women with large wavy hair, heavy bright necklaces and fox collars, and men in well-cut suits and serious, clean faces, smoke dancing up from their American cigarettes more slowly and more preciously than in the outside world.

We sat in a booth by the tinted windows, on two padded leather benches facing each other, drinking vodka and smoking until we were shrouded in a gentle fog. The waitress brought herring in sour cream and Ukrainian borscht with beef, and later a large red snapper for each of us. I felt like I was another person, in another city, leading a careless elevated life. I was surprised by how easily I'd pushed everything else aside, including the meeting with the professor. The vodka helped. The waitress came around and around and filled our glasses without anyone having to remind her. You next to me and Hania opposite, throwing us smiling looks. Maksio recounted one anecdote after another, mostly about girls he had tried to seduce, and you egged him on, teasing him until he told us more, as if you were just like him. I had never seen you like this and was surprised to find that I liked it. In a way, I told myself, it wasn't really you. When I saw Hania staring at you, her eyes wide, mouth open in laughter, I couldn't feel jealousy.

"So you're the reason we haven't seen our Januszek all these weeks," she said at one point, winking at me. "I was beginning to worry some girl had stolen him from us, when really he was just in your sweet company."

You groaned. "Hania, do you have to flirt with all of my friends?"

Maksio and Rafał laughed out loud. I blushed despite myself. Hania rolled her eyes at you and looked at me with complicity.

"How come I never saw you on the field during camp?" I asked, trying to change the mood.

"Excellent question!" Maksio cried. "Sister dear? Why did Your Royal Highness not lift a finger—nor a single beetroot—all summer long?"

Now it was Hania's turn to blush. "Stop teasing me, everyone," she said, affecting irritation, emptying her little glass of vodka and setting it back on the table with a bang that made the neighboring diners look up. "I have delicate hands," she purred, and we laughed.

Dessert arrived, ice cream with chocolate sauce, topped with an absurdly big mountain of whipped cream, served in a tall glass that resembled the trumpet of a flower. It was delicious. I felt like a child again, a happy one this time, whose wishes had always been granted. On the other side of the window night had fallen, and dark figures moved past in the street with downcast faces and empty bags, and empty stomachs, I guessed. But we didn't see them. It was so much better on this side of the glass. So much warmer, so much softer.

We stayed late, until there were almost no other guests. The bill arrived on a small silver platter, and everyone reached for their wallets—or pretended to, in my case—but Maksio waved us off.

"It's on us," he said with a flick of his hand, walking over to the bar, where the waitress stood in front of a wall of foreign alcohols. She smiled at him with deference as he signed the bill and left her a tip.

Outside, in the cool air, we stood and smoked Maksio's Marlboros, smoother than any cigarette I'd ever had. Hania looked around at us, in her catlike observing way, and asked whether we wanted to go to their country house that weekend.

"We'll escape the city, make a little party out of it," she said, her eyes narrowing with satisfaction, her fine mouth curling into a smile.

We all agreed, and kissed one another good night, and

watched them speed off on their Vespa toward their part of town. Rafał waved down a taxi and was gone.

Then it was just you and me on the large empty avenue. We walked uptown. I reached out for your old self, waiting for our masks to wear off in the cold of the night.

"I'm so happy you came," you said, looking at me in a loving, tipsy way, almost childish. "Wasn't it great? What did I tell you, huh?"

I nodded. "It *was* great."

We walked on, the pavements deserted. It was late. I listened out for the sound of our steps. They were almost in unison, and something serious, something important that I'd pushed down all night long, rose to the surface of my mind. I told you about my meeting with the professor, quietly, ashamed about my hopelessness. Not daring to ask anything of you, only recounting. You listened attentively.

We were on Poznańska Street, with its cobbled stones and tall prewar *kamienicas* and lines of prostitutes. Young ones and old ones, most in long coats with miniskirts or tight dresses showing underneath, their bodies violently stretching the fabric, threatening to break it. They called out to us while I talked, accents coarse and loud, and we walked on without looking.

"I'll give you a special price, sweetie," one of them cried with a clipped Silesian twang, "for such a beautiful face. And bring your friend too."

The other women cackled like hyenas in the dark. I didn't dare look at you. I couldn't see anything funny in that moment. We reached the end of the street with the Palace of Culture towering before us, large, dark, and ominous, and beside it the train station, lit but seemingly empty.

You stopped and looked at me with a consolatory smile. "Don't worry, this one is easy. You can ask Hania this weekend. At her house."

A flash of opportunity raced through me. After that night, at the restaurant, anything seemed possible.

"Are you sure?"

You nodded. "She likes you. And I'm sure she can have some strings pulled for you. She and Maksio always had all the exam questions in advance, you know. That's why I never needed to go to lectures. And at the camp neither of them lifted a finger."

I looked at my shoes, my head racing. "And it won't be weird with Hania? Coming on to you?"

You smiled and shook your head lightly. "Did you see her tonight? She's not desperate. Besides, she falls for guys so easily. She's probably into *you* right now." You laughed again.

"OK, then," I said, still anxious. "This weekend."

We hugged, our cheeks coming up against each other, me feeling the beginning of your stubble. I always loved that sensation.

"Good night," you said, turning toward the other side of the river.

"Good night, my dear."

I don't know why I didn't confide in Karolina. Part of me wanted to, longed for someone I could talk to completely. I suppose I wasn't ready. I was afraid she'd smile at me and say, "Hear, hear!" or something cynical about the seductive taste of whisky. I was afraid she'd warn me against asking for favors one couldn't return. The last thing I wanted right then was to be warned. So when I called her that week from a telephone box on the corner of my street and she asked how I was doing, I put on the most cheerful voice I could manage and told her everything was all right. And I let her tell me how she'd fallen for that short boy she'd danced with at Hania's party. His name was Karol. He was an engineer. I made a joke about their names, Karol and Karolina, how it was clearly meant to be, and she laughed, like in the old days. Then she asked me about the PhD. I said I hadn't seen the professor yet, that I was seeing him the week after. That I felt sure I'd get it. She said she'd cross her fingers for me, that she'd be happy for me. Hanging up, I missed her more than I had before the call.

I walked back to the flat to prepare for the weekend away. I packed, unpacked, packed again. Ironed my clothes. It didn't feel like I was going on holiday, but on a mission from which I'd return changed. That evening, just to reassure myself, I walked back down into the cool street and to the telephone box.

"Ludzio, I knew it would be you. Only you would call me so late at night."

She sounded happy.

"Granny."

"How are you getting on, darling?"

I swallowed. "Very well, Granny. Very well."

"Are you sure? Do you need money? You know I have almost nothing, but I set aside a little. I could send you that . . ."

"No, Granny," I said, smiling into the receiver. "I don't need money. It looks like I'm going to do a doctorate. I won't need your help anymore."

"Oh, Ludzio." Her voice sounded teary.

"Are you proud of me, Granny?"

"Of course I am." She sniffed. I leaned my forehead against

the cool metal body of the telephone. "And when will you come home, darling? You know that's what I care about most—seeing you."

"Soon," I said, not sure whether or not it was true. "Soon. When they confirm my doctorate. When I'm settled. I promise."

I hung up, stayed there in the telephone box, in the little halo of the light bulb attached to the ceiling, protected by an iron grid, watching the night outside. My life was a tiny narrow corridor with no doors leading off it, a tunnel so narrow it bruised my elbows, with only one way to go. *That or the void,* I told myself. *That or leave.*

The next day we met at the Square of Three Crosses, on the steps of the domed church that stood in the middle like a pagan temple. It was cold and overcast and overwhelmingly, despairingly gray, one of those particularly Varsovian days that makes you think the sun has ceased to exist and fear that your mind might suffocate underneath an impenetrable fortress of clouds.

You were already there when I arrived, your bag lying by your feet. We kissed each other on the cheek. There was a strange air between us, as if we'd become accomplices in a game. Your eyes sparkled with mischief and play. "Ready?" you said, piercing me with them.

I nodded, feeling a wave of nausea, pushing it away.

Their car arrived on the square. I knew it was theirs before it had even stopped. Foreign cars were so rare even I could tell them apart from the two other kinds that one could dream of owning in our country: it was neither a Maluch, the tin can Fiat made for the socialist bloc, nor the Trabant, the larger, clumsier model from East Germany. Here was a thing as smooth and elegant as a panther—a black Mercedes.

It came to a halt by the steps of the church. The passenger window slid down, and Hania, in a pair of gold-colored sunglasses, waved at us excitedly. "C'mon, boys!"

We grabbed our bags and hurried down. We climbed in, onto the brown leather bench in the back, where Maksio's blonde from the party was already sitting, like a very expensive doll. She wore a short leather miniskirt and a red bandana around her head. Hania introduced her as Agata, and she nodded at us slowly, as if sedated.

"Hey, guys," said Maksio, turning around from the steering wheel with a smile in his eyes. "Let's do this!"

"Is anyone else coming?" I asked.

Hania spun around, her mirrored sunglasses still on, their lenses reflecting and distorting my face, which struck me as silly and pale.

"Just us," she said, and smiled.

We whizzed off, speeding seamlessly and effortlessly along Ujazdowski Avenue. We passed the run-down palaces of the long-forgotten aristocracy, the Łazienki Gardens with my hidden deer, and the gigantic gates and lines of soldiers that protected the castle that was the Soviet embassy. After that the city turned sparse. We passed endless stretches of identical blocks, *blokowisko* upon *blokowisko* with mud fields in between, where riotous hordes of children played. We passed factories, smoking behemoths, big and solemn like sooty churches. The radio was on, playing something by the Velvet Underground. Nico sang in her low, litanic voice about a poor girl and the costumes she'll wear, bells ringing and a guitar jittering, like a flickering mirage.

Throngs of white birch trees came into view, naked in this late autumn and all the more solemn. And fields. Soaked brown fields with women and men and horse-drawn plows. The sky was still covered, white-gray like rice pudding, but in the country-side, among this nature, there was beauty in that, like the comforting duvet in a bed one takes refuge in.

We chatted for some stretches and were silent for others. We rode on and on, rock music playing on the radio, Agata humming along. Light started to drain from the sky, and the earth began to undulate. Low hills surrounded us, and now it was all forest, a sea of pines. And then, at an unmarked dirt road, Maksio turned the car and we drove all the way down through the dense forest until we came to a gate. Hania got out and unlocked it, and we drove through, just as night was falling, along an avenue with tall, stately poplars.

At the end of the lane there was a house. It was white, clear against the dusk like a ghost, with thick, proud columns supporting the triangular roof of the veranda. Leaves and little twigs crunched under our shoes as we climbed out of the car. The house stood there majestically, oblivious to our presence. It was a *dwór*, an old country estate, that must have been there for centuries already and would outlive us all, I thought, and I admired it for that, for all it had already seen and all it would still see that we would never know.

Maksio unlocked the front door, switched on the light inside. The smell of dry cedar invaded my mind. There were old faience stoves, fireplaces, and hunting trophies, the heads of boars and deer, oriental carpets covering the floors. A place of pleasure and peace, indifferent to governments, faithful to whoever happens to be in power. You said something about how impressive it was, this house, and I remained silent, thinking how undeserving you all were of it.

We followed Hania upstairs, where she gave us our room:

you and I would be sharing. She had the room next to ours. Maksio and Agata had taken another bedroom downstairs.

"My parents are coming on Sunday," said Hania, pointing to a large door at the end of the corridor. "That's their room."

"Isn't this house something?" you said as we put down our things and unpacked. "It's practically a castle."

I nodded. I wanted to be alone, to have the place all to myself, to take everything in. There was a view over the garden—a park, really—oblong and wide like several sports fields and bordering the forest. I stood and watched the last specks of light dissolve above it, forgetting myself, until the darkness outside was complete and I could see my face in the window. I turned back to the room. It was large, probably as big as *Pani* Kolecka's little flat. There were two single beds, heavy and gleaming, separated by a nightstand with a porcelain lamp. A door led to a large bathroom with a bathtub. I turned on the tap, enjoyed the savage rumble of the water filling the tub. Steam rose from it. I undressed and got in, leaving the door open to see what I could of the park. The water was too hot, scalding almost, but it embraced me. I lay there for a long time, feeling my skin prickle from the heat, feeling droplets of sweat form on my forehead, letting my mind wander. After a while my eyes closed all by themselves.

When I woke, my body felt cold and suffocated by water. I got out of the bath, my head spinning with hunger, and dried myself with a towel as thick as a *kotlet*. Then I saw that you were gone. I dressed quickly and went downstairs but found no one. I walked around, taking it all in—the dignified wooden furniture, the smell of past fires, the large veranda leading out into the infinite darkness of the garden, the forest a mere silhouette in the distance. And then there were voices, low and hushed. I couldn't tell whose they were. I walked to where I thought they were coming from and found you and Hania in the kitchen. You were standing close together, as if dancing, I thought, but with your arms loose, your faces concentrated and intimate. Hania spoke to you with a smile; you frowned, and then broke into laughter.

"Tell me," I heard her say, teasingly, but you held your sphinx-like smile and shrugged.

As soon as I approached, your heads turned to me in one single movement. And you edged slightly away from her. Her face changed, from intimate to casual.

"There you are!" she cried. "Are you hungry, Ludzio?" I looked at you for an explanation, but it was as if you were in character.

"Starving," I said.

That night, after dinner—roast beef with beetroot mash and apples that Hania had brought from home and warmed up in the oven—we made a fire in the living room, played cards, and drank Bulgarian wine. But the scene I had witnessed between the two of you had pierced my role, made it harder to play. I was distracted, nervous. At the end of the evening, egged on by the rest of us, Agata got up and sang. She sang with real sorrow, a song by Maryla Rodowicz, that quiet, sad song about the old fairgrounds and the tin toys and the balloons. We were all still. Her voice commanded our minds in an unexpectedly sorrowful way.

Not long after, Agata and Maksio went to bed, and then it was only the three of us. Two couches opposite each other, with armchairs on the sides, a low table in the middle. You sat on the couch opposite her, me on one of the armchairs in between. We talked about what we would do the next day. I wanted to go to sleep, and yet I didn't want to leave you two alone. Then you announced you were going to bed and looked at me meaningfully, as if to say this was my chance. I didn't move. We bid you good night, Hania and I. She smiled and looked out into the dark garden, or maybe at her reflection in the glass. Then she glanced at me. There was tension around her lips.

"I'm so glad you've come," she said. She seemed nervous, and this surprised me.

"Thank you for having me," I said. "It's wonderful here."

"Of course." She nodded and looked toward the garden again, as if deciding something.

"I hope I'm not being indiscreet, but—" She stopped, looked at her lap, then at me again. "Allow me to ask you something personal."

I said nothing, trying to stave off internal vertigo.

"I don't mean to pry." She shifted, visibly uncomfortable, vulnerable even, but not nearly as much as me. "Tell me honestly—does Janusz have another girl?"

A part of me wanted to laugh out loud, hysterically, until my throat, vocal cords, and stomach muscles hurt. The other part didn't, was just plain exhausted. I kept my face neutral, shook my head truthfully.

"No. You don't need to worry about that."

"Really?" Her face changed, lightened. "It's just . . . he's so distant sometimes. And I don't understand why he's not really responding to me. You see what I mean . . . ?" Her eyes asked for reassurance.

I looked at my fingers and nodded.

"Does he ever mention me?" she probed.

"Yes," I said, ungenerously, wishing I could help her. "Yes, he does."

She seemed hopeful but unconvinced, her widened eyes revealing her need for more.

"Does he *like* me? Has he said anything to you?"

I swallowed. Vertigo, this time lucid, took hold of me.

"I don't know," I said, aware that it was the truth. "He hasn't told me. You'll have to ask him."

The next morning I awoke with a headache, bothered by the sunlight that came into the room. Your bed was made, and you were gone. I took a shower and went downstairs, where all of you were sitting at the long table in the dining room. Hania and Agata both had wet hair, combed back, and the air smelled of coffee. You were eating a roll with two slices of ham. "There he is!" said Maksio when I entered, and everyone looked up and greeted me sleepily. Hania was sitting beside you.

After breakfast we all went for a walk through the forest. It was damp—it had rained during the night—and smelled of freshness and decomposition. We walked on layers and layers of fallen leaves and the last of the autumn's mushrooms. I tried to talk to Hania then, but we were never alone. And somehow I was glad about that. The day was too bright, and I knew I'd need alcohol to do it.

That afternoon Hania said she was preparing a surprise for us; after lunch she and Agata went out with two empty baskets. The three of us stayed behind in the house. You and Maksio played billiards downstairs, and I went up to our room. Upstairs it was completely quiet. Before I reached our room, my eyes fell on the double door at the end of the corridor, and a dark curiosity overcame me. I listened for a sound—there was nothing. I moved toward the door and pushed down the handle. It wasn't locked. My heart beating hard, I slipped in. It was a large room with a fantastic view over the park. There was a four-poster bed, perfectly made, the air around it strangely solemn and untouchable, like the bed of someone recently deceased. I walked to the window, took in its view over the forest. Right by the window stood a shiny round table covered in framed photos: Hania and Maksio as children, chubby and small, but the same faces, eating ice cream; their parents—the father like an older, fatter version of Maksio, though with a different mouth, almost lipless, and the mother, tall and elegant, with Hania's dark eyes. A more recent one of the four of them standing and smiling with the Eiffel Tower behind them. And then my eyes fell on the photograph beside that one, and for a moment I saw without comprehending. My mind jarred. In it, their father was dressed in a military uniform, covered in honors and medals. My own hands were shaking as I took the photo from the table and looked at it up close. I felt nauseous, dirty even. Hania's father and Gierek, shaking hands, smiling at each other.

The Party Secretary's face was broad, self-satisfied, taking in Hania's father with apparent fondness. The same man who'd looked down on me from countless banners and posters during the parades, the country's so-called savior. The one who'd ordered the price increases. I thought of the empty shops across the country, of *Pani* Kolecka, of the lives spent queuing for little or nothing—and then these smiles, fat and self-indulgent. I was dumbstruck. I wanted to throw the photo to the ground, to stomp on it, to feel the glass and wood shatter beneath my heel. To hear the paper rip, to see their smiles tear apart. It was only with great effort that I made myself put down the photo and walk back to our room. I lay on my bed, my eyes open. The whole scheme—to ask Hania for help with my doctorate—now seemed more obscene than ever, and yet I told myself that I had to do it. *Just this one time, ask for this one thing, and then never deal with them again.* I closed my eyes, and the world spun around me, my weight shifting and spinning with it.

When I opened my eyes, the room was dark. I felt pleasantly dulled. Night had fallen outside. Laughter came from downstairs, and I heard footsteps in the corridor. You opened the door with an expression of barely suppressed excitement.

"It's dinnertime," you said, looking at me. "Are you coming?"

I nodded. "I'll be down in a minute."

I washed my face and put on a clean white shirt. When I came downstairs something was already in full swing. A record was playing, and you were all in the kitchen, wineglasses on the counter, you talking to Maksio, and Agata and Hania hunched over a pot on the stove. There was a strong earthy smell in the air.

"What's for dinner?" I asked.

Maksio looked up and smiled mischievously. "Hania's witch specialty," he said. "Not especially filling, but you won't feel any hunger—trust me."

Agata chuckled; Hania threw him an indulgent look and turned to me with a long wooden spoon in her hand. She was wearing a purple wrap dress, and a huge amber pendant hung from her neck.

"It's a special soup I make from time to time," she said, a smile playing on her lips. "I think you'll like it."

"Either way, we need to make the most of tonight," said Maksio, looking irritated. "Tomorrow the 'rentals are coming."

"Our *parents* are coming tomorrow," said Hania without turning around. "But just for one night. They won't be bothering us." She took a large porcelain bowl and poured the soup in. It was the color of mud, dark and rich. "However, we won't be able to do *this*. So let's eat."

We sat down at the table with the large bowl in the middle. Its earthy smell wafted up with the steam. Everyone looked expectant and excited, even Agata.

"What *is* this?" I asked.

Hania looked around the group, everyone smiling at my question. "*Zupa*," she said, meaningfully. "Poppy-stem soup. It will send you flying."

Her black eyes gleamed. You were sitting next to her and nodded at me encouragingly. She served me the first cup and handed it across the table. All eyes were on me. I held the cup to my lips and downed it in its entirety, pouring it into myself like medicine. I wanted to dissolve with it. There was a dark-brown taste to it, bitter, unforgiving. They smiled at me and followed my lead, all drinking too. We sat around looking at one another, Hania rubbing my hand across the table, giggling. You held her hand and Maksio's hand. We all took one another's hands and formed a chain. And moments later—or was it more than that?—we were all sitting on the couches, spread out, joyous. My body was weightless. There was nothing on my mind, nothing at all; it was so light it floated. I saw you sitting near me, and all I felt was love. I closed my eyes and saw fields, and flowers, and the lake, the lake from that summer, and everything was there for me, only for me, and I loved myself—all of it, every atom—like I never had before. The music that was playing was the most beautiful thing I'd ever heard. Every word of it—it was Serge Gainsbourg singing in French—I understood. It carried messages I had never expected there were. And we danced. You and me, Hania and you, me and her. Agata and Maksio. All of us together.

I was warm, so warm. The fire was burning, heat enveloped us, and we started to undress, dreamlike, entranced. Looking at one another, like children, without a trace of shame. One by one, clothes fell to the ground—jeans and skirts and shirts and blouses, socks and pants. Until we were all naked, the air on our white bodies, the night around our pale skin. We were an army of erotic ghosts. And we were all beautiful. Hania and Agata with their dark triangles between their thighs and their breasts like overripe fruit, Agata rounder and softer than Hania, whose skin was translucent, blindingly white, a Venus and a nymph. Maksio, his fleshy body like Samson, a colossus, his penis massive like a bull's, his chest hairy and broad like a drum. But you were the most beautiful of them all. Your body was made of marble and absorbed the light of the moon.

Agata opened the veranda and we ran outside, like children on midsummer night. We didn't feel the cold, only the embrace of the night air on our skin. It was like swimming, dipping into the air. Our arms outstretched, reaching for the moon.

"Let's play hide-and-seek!" cried Hania, taking a cloth from the garden table, blindfolding Maksio. We turned him around and around, our fingers on his waist and hips, his penis swinging along with the turns, our hands slapping his backside.

"Count to thirty!"

We ran into the garden, into the forest. The girls in one direction, you and I in another. Grass and twigs tickled our feet.

"You can take off your blindfold now!" Hania's voice called from far away.

You and I behind a tree, somewhere by the edge of the forest. Our hands on the bark, beginning to freeze, and then finding warmth, our arms around each other. Our bodies formed one, protecting each other from the cold, perfect in the night. We kissed. You were mine. I realized then that this was the only thing that counted. Nothing else had ever existed. Just our lips and hips and sighs. I fell into different galaxies through you, your mouth a porthole to a better universe, and then the cracking of twigs behind us and there was Maksio, standing naked a couple of meters away, looking at us with his mouth wide open. His eyes dilated, his body frozen.

I could sense a quiver of fear run through your body. You tried to say something, but Maksio, completely out of nowhere, started to laugh. He laughed out loud like a crazed bear. It seemed like his laughter would bring the forest down, make the pines shed their needles.

Your face lightened up suddenly, and you laughed too. "It was a joke!" you cried, concentrating, looking at him. "Ludwik challenged me. I lost a bet."

Maksio stopped laughing, his eyes flickering between you and me.

The girls emerged from behind the trees. "What happened?" asked Agata. "Why were you laughing?"

Maksio turned around to them and started walking away. "Nothing," he said. "A hallucination. I won."

We walked back to the veranda, and I couldn't look at you, only at the ground, not sure what had just happened. I was hot. I was burning. I was entirely aflame. Then it was the next round and my turn to be blindfolded. I laughed and laughed as they spun me, despite myself, and I counted to thirty, cold and dizzy when I opened my eyes and they were gone. I walked into the forest, and there were Maksio and Agata, kissing in a clearing. I tapped them on the shoulder. They looked up, smiled, and continued their embrace. "I'll find the other two!" I cried, running farther into the forest, over fallen trunks and little valleys. I ran until I was lost, until I was sure I'd lost you. I tried to find my way back. The forest had started to close in on me, to turn from enchanting to threatening. It felt like a nightmare, and I knew my mind wasn't working clearly. I stopped, tried to calm myself. Then an owl hooted somewhere behind me and I turned. Whiteness glowed behind a tree, like a luminescent stone in the sea. I walked toward it, fast, my heart beating with imminent success. And then I saw the different shades of white—darker white on lighter white, matted marble on chalk. Two bodies on the forest floor, legs entwined. I stood, watching your feet move over each other, soles black with earth and leaves, writhing, struggling. There was cruelty in those round forms on top of each other—you over her, your chest over hers, her closed eyes lit by the moonlight. I turned back and ran. I ran and started to shiver all over, like a child who's broken through ice and fallen into a lake and only just managed to crawl out. I ran and ran, becoming completely and utterly numb, not feeling a thing. Not feeling the cold, not feeling my lungs, only terror propelling me forward. It felt like, if only I ran fast enough, all this would not be true—that the farther I ran, the farther I would be from what I'd seen.

When I got to the house, Maksio and Agata were there, looking at me as if I were a ghost, asking me questions I couldn't hear. I only saw their mouths moving. I thought I would suffocate or faint. It was as if I hadn't breathed at all during my run, as if I hadn't breathed in years. There I stood and felt my head deflating, my whole being draining of air, and I began to pant like a horse after a race. I bent over, hands on my knees, trying not to drown in the emptiness, the vacuum of myself. But something inside was broken, no doubt about it.

"Are you OK?" asked Maksio.

I saw then that they were dressed again. I had never felt so naked in my life, so utterly vulnerable. I shook my head. Then the lights went out.

I remember I vomited during the night, convulsively. It felt like I was setting something free, ridding myself of a monster. I remember nothing else, apart from the feeling that I wasn't in control of my body. The thought went through my mind that I might die. That I didn't have the strength or the wits to do anything about it. That I just had to let it happen—whatever "it" was going to be. And then, like something heavy and wet sliding into a black hole in the ground, I fell asleep again.

When I woke I didn't know who I was. My mind was a clean slate, for just one beautiful moment. Until the memory came crashing down. I was lying in the bed in our room upstairs, naked under the covers. My guts and head were burning. The curtains were drawn. Faint sunlight glowed underneath and around their edges. You in the other bed, asleep. Your shoulder moved almost imperceptibly, your breathing inaudible. I pulled myself up. My body was heavy and unfamiliar; every movement felt unusual. I put on some clothes, threw the rest of my things into my bag. You didn't stir as I walked out. I moved across the silent corridor, over the oriental carpets, downstairs to the room with the fireplace. It was cool. Empty bottles on tables, the faded smell of cigarettes. And in the middle of the room, like some bizarre offering, was a mound made up of our clothes. Outside on the veranda there was a burned spot where a fire had been. Birds—small and fat, with orange beaks—flew around excitedly, picking at something in the dewy grass. A pair of panties. White and lacy, discarded like someone's fantasy.

I walked out through the front door, left it open behind me—across the gravel path, through the open gate at the end of the poplared avenue. The trees and the dirt road already made me feel as if I were breathing more lightly. The sun was still coming up, sending butter-colored light across the park. And I was so glad to be on this path by myself. So endlessly glad. But just when I was about to reach the road, a black limousine with tinted windows came toward me. I kept my head down, accelerated my steps, hoping it wouldn't stop, hoping Hania's parents—was that who was in there?—wouldn't interrogate me. The car passed without stopping or slowing down, gravel crunching beneath its massive wheels. I reached the main road. Breathing in and out, I reveled in the emptiness. Then a church bell rang in the distance, and I decided to find it. I walked along the forest road. Horse-drawn carts with families passed by, and the ringing of the bell became more distinct. Not long after, a village appeared, along with the church. It was wooden and old, its spire almost black. People streamed in, families, old people, children in hordes. I followed them into the darkness inside. The organ was playing, and a soothing cloud of heavy incense hung in the air.

I stood among boys and young men in suits, some with unruly hair, many with heavy, broad faces, burned and weathered, blue eyes, caps in their hands held in front of their crotches. Whenever a woman came in, another boy would get up from the benches, shooed by his mother, and stand with us men, letting the woman pass. No one seemed to notice me. I was invisible in the crowd. The priest stepped up to the pulpit in white-and-purple robes, greeting the congregation. Then the organ started up again and everyone began to sing. The notes moved slowly through space and through the crowd, elevated, unified us, passed through the single body of us and up to the murky windows and the dark ceiling. Tears gathered in my eyes, releasing themselves. I joined in the singing.

CHAPTER 7

WINTER CAME EARLY THAT year. Every week pulled us deeper into its gloom, every day shorter than the last, as if time was running out. What surprised me most was how calm I was. Maybe it was the drugs. Maybe I was still in another drug-infused dimension, preternaturally wise. Or maybe it was shock. Or denial. Maybe the whole thing was just too big to comprehend. Or it didn't mean anything yet. There were moments when I wanted to lie on the ground and feel the street's concrete against my face. Just lie down, stop. To feel a heavy weight on me, feel my bones crack, feel myself drift off to sleep, forever. But all this I pushed back.

Amid the chaos in my mind, I knew that I could not continue my life as it had been. I knew I had to leave. I tried to think of only that. And so, on a terribly gray and cold morning, I went to the Passport Bureau. It was a tall brown building in a side street in the center of the city, not too far from the National Museum, where the strikes had been. I went with trembling hands, pushing away the memory of the night I'd released the flyers, my story assembled in my head. I sat in the cold hall, filling out the forms, strangely aware of my handwriting and, like whenever I had to supply the official data of my life, feeling as if I were lying. The form asked where I was going, for how long and why, and I stuck to my story.

For what felt like days, I sat in the dark and drab halls of the Bureau, on a hard, wooden bench, holding a piece of paper with a number, waiting for it to be my turn.

I sat in the hallway and tried not to cry. I wanted to cease existing. I wanted to un-be. I sat in the hallway and tried not to think of you and me. I tried not to think of us, under the covers of your bed. I tried not to think of your arms or your hands or your eyes. I tried not to think of all the things I had imagined we'd do together—return to our lake next summer, move in together someday. I tried not to think of Hania, and your fingers on her sequined dress. I tried not to think of Maksio or his eyes when he saw us in the forest. I tried not to think of Granny or Professor Mielewicz.

I tried to imagine my life in the future, in a year or so. I couldn't see anything. I couldn't see anything because anything that wasn't that moment—no, not even that—was beyond me. I started rocking my legs and feet, just to feel something. And then the office closed before my number was called. I left with nothing to show for my time except the flimsy piece of paper whose handwritten number had smudged from my holding it for too long.

I went home. I would get used to it, *Pani* Kolecka told me. She made us a sparse dinner, buckwheat with pickled cucumbers and beetroot mash, and we ate with the windows open, the cold drifting in, stirring us, the sound of cars rushing past in the streets.

"We're just queuing for a possibility, queuing for something, maybe queuing for nothing," she said, smiling her sad and loving smile. "But it will pass, my dear. Even the longest queue dissolves eventually."

The next day I went back to the Bureau. I sat and waited, among rows of others, young and old and ageless, all silent, all torpid, reading or knitting or fiddling with their clothes with unnatural resigned slowness, while the large clock ticked and numbers were called out every now and then by a plaintive voice. My body hurt from the bench. I was hungry. But, bizarrely, I remained calm. The calm, I think, was still a form of shock. If I had let anything out, it all would have overwhelmed me. The fear, the terror of my life alone, was always there, like a clasping, growing abyss, waiting to devour me. I can still feel the tremors of that fear today, its echoes firmly anchored under my fingertips and in that small, weightless space inside my lower belly, just inches above the verge of my crotch.

At the end of the day, my number was called. I walked down the corridor, my footsteps echoing on the stone floor. I knocked on a door, my pulse thumping in my ears. I obeyed the voice that said, "Come in."

The office was narrow and long and dim. I had to walk half a dozen steps to reach the desk, and I strained my eyes to see the man in a tiny patch of lamplight—a bald man with black-rimmed glasses.

"Take a seat," he said, his voice formal but not unfriendly. "I'm just finishing something."

I sat in the chair opposite him. He was bent over some files, absorbed in their contents. His desk was covered in piles of them, neatly stacked blocks of paper. There was only the sound of a clock ticking, slowly, unwillingly.

"So," the man said, looking up at me, somewhat weary, bags under his eyes behind his glasses. He opened another file, which I assumed was mine. His eyes scurried over it, moving quickly, and second by second his expression hardened. I thought he'd ask me questions about my trip. I had my story ready—that I was going to visit an uncle in Chicago over Christmas and that I'd be back in January. I expected him to ask why I had never gone to visit my family before, how I could possibly afford the trip, and how they could possibly know I wouldn't defect. I thought he'd launch into the standard lecture about the dangers of the capitalist world, how they were the enemies of socialism, and how I should never speak to foreigners about politics, except to praise the advance and success of socialist Poland. This is what people had said always happened. But none of that happened. Instead, he set down the file after a moment and looked at me with an expression that was impossible to read.

"We know about you, citizen," he said, with an expectant look. "We *know* about you."

I couldn't breathe. The night of the flyers, the window, the faces staring up at me. Who'd told them? Had they been following me all along? I couldn't make a sound. The man looked satisfied.

"We know about your deviancy, about your pederasty." He said the words clinically, with a detached sort of judgment, the way I imagined he would have said "treason." All feeling left my body, as if my cells were deserting me. It was as if someone had hurled me into a vortex, with no up and no down, nothing to hold on to. No one had ever said these things to me. Something private, something utterly unspoken yet essential, was being ripped out of me. I couldn't say anything. Maybe they were baiting me, I thought, maybe I could argue my way out of this. But I was unable to think or maneuver; I was caught in the jaws of something much too powerful, something that paralyzed me from within. Satisfaction flickered across his face—a face that could have been anyone's, an unremarkable, everyday face.

"I don't know what you're talking about," I said, knowing I could never carry through with this.

His face didn't change. He looked back at the file. "Does the name Marian Zalewski mean anything to you?"

I shook my head truthfully.

With his eyes on the file, he continued. "Zalewski was caught in the Staromiejski Park in Wrocław over three years ago—April the twenty-third, 1977. Engaging in sodomy with another citizen." He looked back at me. "He obediently gave to us the names of others like him. All the names he knew. All contained in a statement, signed by him personally. One of them was yours."

He took something out of the file and handed it to me. It was a photograph, passport-size. It showed the face of an old man I had never seen before, staring straight into the camera. His face was deeply lined and hollow. Dried, emptied of life. And then, in a flash, I recognized him: it was the man from the park bench, from the night I'd run away from home. The man who'd told me his life story, the man whose mouth had relieved my anxiety for one night—and whom I had told my name. Instead of anger, a strange sort of tenderness invaded me. He looked so sad, so forsaken in the photo. Fury awoke in me on his behalf. I could see him being dragged out of the park, into the back of a police van; I could see him sitting in some cold underground office, beaten, blackmailed, made to sign this statement that now lay neatly before a bureaucrat.

"What does this have to do with my passport?" I asked, impatient. "Will you give it to me or not?"

He put down the file slowly and folded his hands over it, retaining his calm.

"That depends entirely on you, citizen. On you and your common sense." He closed my file, placed his elbows on it, and looked at me with narrowed eyes, his pupils small and intense, like the heads of nails. "If you want your passport, you will do the same thing Comrade Marian did: supply us with names. And dates. And circumstances."

He pulled out a piece of blank paper from his desk drawer and pushed it across the table toward me.

"Write."

At first, there was emptiness. Thoughts flew through space, trying to ignite. A sky readied for fireworks, a stage cleared for decisions. But where do decisions come from?

I saw you and Hania slung together, dancing, oblivious to me on the other side of the window. My stomach began to burn, secreting pain like arrowheads, and then the two of you as a four-legged creature, struggling on the forest floor. Eating itself, aware only of itself. At the same time your pleas for trust rang in my ears, your pleas for my patience. The fire in my belly spread. My back reached for soreness, my eyes stirred and dampened. The man was still there, staring at me. And so was the piece of paper.

I felt the pause of time. A moment pulled into its smallest parts, spread so thin it threatened to break. When I imagined taking that piece of paper and reaching for the pen, pictured the possibility of it, of writing your name, my arm refused to move. I couldn't feel it. I couldn't feel the fire in my gut; I couldn't feel any pain. I'd gone numb.

I don't know what took over then, in the void of the next

moment. I guess it wasn't anything distinct, more a hazy murmur, an animal voice, instinct. I followed what it said—what I
could make out, anyway. I knew it spoke the truth. I opened my
mouth. My body felt heavy, absurd, like two fur coats worn at
once.

"No," I said to the man's stony face. "I don't have any names."

It wasn't easy—he was determined to get what was his. But
I knew to persist, knew to take his mounting threats as a sign
of progress. I ignored him when he said I would never leave
the country in my life and never find a job if I didn't comply. I
ignored him when he turned aggressive and called me a pervert
and a sick fuck. To my own surprise, I was unable to accept the
shame he wanted me to feel. It was too familiar to be imposed:
I had produced it myself for such a long time that, right then,
I found I had no space left for it anymore. Instead, I used the
truth. I said that I'd been drugged the week before and that my
mind was addled, the past like a blur. I don't know whether he
believed me. But finally, I can't be sure why, he told me I had
two days. Two days to come up with names. Before he released
me, he put his hands on his desk and said, with a voice measured and sharp like a scalpel, that I would regret it for the rest
of my life if I didn't turn up. I nodded and walked out, feeling
nothing. Outside, night had fallen. I breathed in the winter air.
I knew where I had to go.

The tram rumbled across the bridge. The trees lining the banks
of the river were naked, their leaves having fallen into the water, swept away by the current. The Madonna in the courtyard
was covered with a layer of frost, the yellow gladiolas gone. Every step on the staircase was an effort. Every creaking one, I

thought, would alert you to my presence. There were no children playing, no people outside—just me and the dark old wood of the house. I knocked on your door, my body a mere shell. My heart beating as if I'd climbed the Tatra range. I wasn't even sure why I'd come.

You opened the door, and a ripple passed over your face. As if it didn't know what to express. Right then it showed nothing but determined strength. You looked at me. I looked back, trying to gauge the moment, feeling out of control. You seemed so much taller then, standing above me, looking down.

I thought we would stand like this forever. I thought I was too proud to even begin to speak, that I would not beg for anything, that I had no reason to feel sorry. But looking at you softened me—despite your new hardness, or because of it. It hurt to see you like that, to have nothing pass between us. Then I saw something in your eyes, an opening.

"Aren't you going to let me in?" I said.

You stepped away from the door, opening the way for me.

It had never been so cold in your room. The heater—a contraption of conjoined white pipes, right by the door—was banging and clanging, as if there were a dwarf trapped inside, whacking around with a stick. I was glad I had my coat. I noticed then that you were wearing a thick sweater and a scarf. You closed the door behind me.

"So you came." It sounded as if you were saying it more to yourself than to me. You stood by the door, looked at me, somewhat helpless in the middle of the room. "Sit."

There was nowhere to sit but on the bed. It was neatly made and covered with several blankets. On the desk, by the window, lay open books and a writing pad. I sat on the very edge of the bed, feeling the blankets underneath me, feeling a void where certainty had once been. You stood by the door, your arms crossed over your chest, looking at me.

"Why did you run away?" There was reproach and a hint of pain in your voice.

The question took me by surprise. I thought there'd be small talk; I thought we would dance around what we really felt. I swallowed, searched for something true and worth putting into words.

"It was too much," I said, unable to look at you. "And—" It seemed unsayable to me; continuing was like jumping through fire.

You looked straight at me. "What?"

I hesitated. And in that hesitation, resentment came through.

"That night. When Maksio saw us. What you said to him. And later, I saw you. In the forest. With Hania."

I closed my eyes, exhausted. I didn't want to see your reaction. But I looked up anyway. Your face was hard again, in a different way. Your jaw stiff, your eyes staring at the floor, hooded from me. Suddenly I felt trapped, seized by a desire to run away. You looked up toward me, your eyes rueful, shimmering.

"We were all on drugs, Ludzio. You never should have seen us. It didn't mean anything. It was a game. It was innocent."

You looked at me for a reaction. *This has never been a game,* I thought, *and never innocent either.* But I couldn't bring myself to say it. It seemed as if we'd entered a realm where words had lost their meaning. I just looked at you, saw you struggle, harden again at my silence.

"You could have said something before leaving," you said, reproachful now. "We could have talked about it. You didn't even give me a chance to explain. And now you've ruined it for yourself. With her. Can you imagine that we were worried about you? That we thought you might have run into the forest and be in need of help?" You looked genuinely pained, and for a moment I felt guilty. "Luckily her parents told us that they'd seen you. They obviously think you're crazy. What are you going to do now? Huh?"

I looked at you, for the first time, I think, with pity. "We're beyond that now," I said softly. "I'm leaving."

The words were like a spell, suspending whatever we'd said before. Fear grazed your face, made your eyes search mine for signs.

"Where to?" you asked, almost in disbelief.

"The States."

Realization spread like water on paper. Your mouth defeated, your eyes averted. I hated to see you like this.

"Did they give you a passport?" you asked quietly, without any intonation at all. I remained still.

"Not yet."

You nodded, looking at the floor, then toward the window. I wanted you to say more. I felt as if I had no more weapons left. You walked to the window, didn't look at me. Breathed heavily.

"Won't you come?" I asked, feeling foolish as soon as I'd said it.

You laughed: a quick, short exhalation of a laugh, one that didn't go with your eyes. They were bitter.

"Why do you need to leave?" you said, turning to me. "We were so close to getting what we wanted."

I considered you, breathed in deeply, closed my eyes for a moment, opened them again.

"We weren't, Janusz. You just thought we were. Don't you see what this is doing to us? It's humiliating."

You looked straight back at me. "More humiliating than living in a freezing attic, like a rat? Or than working hard your whole life and getting nothing for it? I thought you wanted a better life than that."

"I do," I said, feeling cold. "I do."

You sat on your desk, back turned to the window, your face collapsing into your hands. And I felt tenderness, a possibility. I stood, walked over to you, put my hand on your shoulder. I could feel the tension of your muscles through the wool.

"Come with me," I whispered. "It's not too late. We could go without anyone knowing, across the mountains to Czechoslovakia, then on to Austria. No one will know us there."

"We'd have nothing," you insisted from beneath your hands. "We don't speak the language. We'd be lost."

"We'd be free."

The room was so filled with us, with the gathering clouds of our words, the fog of our thoughts. I lifted my hand off you.

"Think of *Giovanni's Room*," I said, the story returning to me through the fog. "Think of how David leaves Giovanni out of fear. We mustn't act out of fear."

You withdrew your hands from your flushed face, staring not at me but through me. "It's too much." Your voice was tired. "I can't do it, Ludzio. I can't. You're asking for too much."

"Is it because of Hania?" I felt my head spin with fear.

You didn't say anything, looked down, your face still flushed, not moving. "It's not that easy," you finally said. Somehow, I believed you.

"Remember how David feels after his decision," I said, feeling my throat tighten. "He regrets it."

"Stop comparing us to that book!" Your voice shattered

against the walls. Your face was distorted, scrunched up be-yond recognition. *"You're* the one who wants to run off. *You're* the one trying to force me into this. You can't make people love you the way you want them to."

I felt life drain out of me, as if a plug had been pulled. I sat down on the bed.

"I'm not cut out for it, Ludwik," you said, like an apology. "I belong here. And I will make it, one way or another." You got up from the desk, stepping toward me with new confidence. "I met Hania's parents. I got on with her dad. He will help me move up. I'm sure of it." There was hope in your voice. You al-most sounded as if you wanted me to be proud of you. I said nothing. You were only a meter away; I could have touched you if I'd reached out. "And maybe it's not too late for you either," you went on. "Maybe we can speak to Hania, maybe Maksio will never mention what he saw, and—"

I stood.

"I need to go," I said, knowing it was true. Your face, your limbs—it was as if your entire being was trying to hold itself together, almost shaking from the effort of it. I couldn't bear to see it. I averted my eyes and slid to the door like some retreat-ing thief, stopping in my tracks when you called my name.

It sounded like an appeal, a right violated and invoked. My hand on the door handle, my back to you, my heart pulsing in my temples. I could sense the word throbbing in the air. My name, claiming me. It wrapped its fingers around my shoulders and tried to hold me back. With a terrible jolt I thrust open the door and hurried down the dark of the stairs.

The night had grown colder. The street was empty. The light of the streetlamps was dim, and the cursing of invisible drunk

men and women pierced the air. I knew you wouldn't come after me, and most of me didn't want you to. But without knowing why, I began to run, fueled by some kind of elated panic. I
ran as fast as I could on the frosted pavements, alongside the
battered buildings, across a naked square. I ran without stopping, feeling the cold sting my lungs, feeling it rush through my
head and out. Through the warren of the cobbled streets, past
the golden dome of the Orthodox church, straight on toward the
bridge. I ran until feeling returned to my body, until my legs
became heavy, until the pain began to prickle and I was out of
options, out of breath. When I stopped, I was standing on the
bridge, clutching a rail, bent over like an upturned L. I drew in
deep, hot, thorny breaths. My head was spinning. I closed my
eyes. I held on tighter to the rail, much tighter. Until I sank to
my knees and cried out in pain and felt the cold, hard concrete
push against me.

Later, when the spinning had stopped, the tremor had receded,
and the cold of the ground had seeped into my bones and I
knew it wouldn't save me, that maybe nothing could, I opened
my eyes and heaved myself up. The city lay before me oddly
turned away from the river, oddly calm. The houses of the Old
Town perched on the hill, the sharp spire of the palace to the
left, the *blokowiskos* discernible behind. In the dark of that night
it all seemed barely real.

Looking back, I'm surprised I didn't hurl myself off the
bridge. I was terrified, saw no way out. But I suppose that right
then, in the midst of despair, I felt the stirring of instinct again,
the murmur of that voice. I brushed the dirt off my clothes and
walked home with a rising fever. Somehow I knew that something would occur to me, a pact I could try to live with.

That night, plagued by hot flashes and frenetic dreams, I got out of bed and stood by the window of my little room. Outside, the city was a ghost filled with comatose trees. For a moment I thought of you in your room, calling my name as I left. I thought of all the times you had lied, trying to straddle her and me. It was then that the idea occurred to me. I knew, without having to think twice, that there was no other way.

The next morning I left early. I walked from the same spot where we'd met that night, along the avenue by the Łazienki Gardens, its trees and bushes leafless and naked now. How did my deer cope? I found the side street with the large *kamienica*. I pressed the button on the intercom.

"Hello?" Her voice clear and untainted.

"It's Ludwik," I said.

"Oh." Surprise in her voice, a little pause. "Come on up."

I took the lift, observed my burdened face in the mirror. The last time I'd been there with you felt like a lifetime ago.

The door to the flat was open as I came out of the lift. Hania stood beside it, with a conciliatory smile that pained me. She was wearing a sweater, a long red skirt, and thick socks. We kissed on the cheek.

"It's good to see you," she said softly, and again I believed her, as I had every time she'd said it. I could hardly muster the strength to go in. The flat looked lighter and bigger than I remembered. We walked through to the splendid living room where the party had been, now flooded by winter light. She made me sit on the white couch.

"Would you like something to drink? Grapefruit juice?" She frowned, sensing my nervousness, maybe. "Some brandy?"

I shook my head.

She sat down, her long skirt falling from couch to carpet.

"I need to apologize to you," she said, looking at me ruefully. "About the night in the country. I'm sorry the *zupa* was so strong. I feel terrible about the whole thing. It all went too far, and it was my fault." She looked embarrassed.

"It's OK," I said, feeling relieved. "You didn't know. I'm sorry for taking off without a word."

I tried to smile. She nodded, as if she'd understood.

There was silence for a moment, in which I felt my pulse quicken.

"I came to ask you a favor," I heard myself say. I couldn't look at her, so I looked at my interlaced fingers, which I'd been pressing so hard they'd turned red and white. "I'm in trouble. I need your help."

Her eyes widened, and she gave me a nod, as if to say, "Go on."

I told her about the man in the office. The words came out more easily than before. I chose them carefully. I told her I wanted to leave to see my uncle. That they were holding on to my passport, blackmailing me—though I didn't go into detail. I avoided the question for as long as I could, absurdly, and she let me go on. Light shone onto the parquet, making it look smooth and perfect, like the surface of an ice rink. Hania looked at me with concern and sympathy all the way through, and strangely, despite myself, despite all my instincts of pain and revenge and humiliation for having to ask her, of all people, I felt a surge of love for her gentleness, her kindness in listening to me. For her ignorance of all that had happened between you and me. And for my innocence as seen through her eyes. When I finished talking, she put her hand on my shoulder, a hand that weighed almost nothing, and said:

"I will talk to my father."

I thanked her but saw that there was something unresolved in her face. She turned toward the large windows, toward the white winter sun. Then she pulled her legs up off the floor and folded them against herself, embracing them and her skirt.

"There's just one thing I need to know," she said slowly, looking uncomfortable. "What they are blackmailing you with. It will help. To know how to best approach the situation."

I tried to concentrate on breathing. It felt like I was falling. I couldn't possibly.

"Ludwik?"

"They know that I'm . . ." I couldn't face her eyes, couldn't say it. Had never said it to anyone. Not even to myself. It felt like jumping over a five-meter wall.

"Tell me," she said gently, her weightless hand on my shoulder again. "Go on. Don't be scared."

I almost crumbled. I took on the words again, as if they had fallen to the floor. I picked them up, lifted them, tried to push them over the threshold, like something immensely heavy that could crush me.

"I'm a . . ." I tried and failed under her gaze.

It was the same feeling, the same pulling to and fro, one feels when standing on the edge of a diving board.

"I'm a—" My voice almost steady. "I'm a homosexual."

The world did not tumble. Her face remained calm. The white winter light still streamed into the room as if into a church, illuminating the floor and us, my heart pumped blood around my body—accelerated but still—and a shiver ran through me, through my entire being, and I felt as if something dead and heavy inside had been expelled, as if I'd been carrying a leaden ghost within me all that time. I felt dizzy. I tried to say something else, but there was nothing to say. She took me into her arms, and I allowed her to—into her soft arms, against her pull-over, cushioned by the soft breasts beneath it.

"It's OK," she whispered. "I understand." She stroked my hair. "You're good. Don't you worry. You'll be fine. You're good."

Even if I had wanted to, I wouldn't have been able to stop the tears. They poured out all by themselves, a force of their own, agents of relief and consolation, flooding my face, empty-ing my mind. And we sat like this, enveloped in each other, in the bright light, for an immeasurable amount of time. When I straightened myself, she left, returning moments later with a tissue.

I wiped my face and thanked her.

She stood still, looking down at me.

"You love him, don't you?"

She said it softly, neutral, almost as if it wasn't a question. I closed my eyes to say yes and looked at her, saw that she'd understood. Then a shadow flickered across her face, a trace of doubt. The moment I'd been sure would come. She remained still and looked at me intently, scanning me for reassurance, begging me for it with her eyes.

"You and Janusz—" she began, but I interrupted her.

"He doesn't know," I said, slipping the wet ball of tissue into my pocket, trying not to tremble, to keep my voice steady. "Don't say anything to him."

She nodded, her fear dissolved. "Of course not," she said, try-ing to cover her relief. "I won't."

She offered me brandy again, asked me whether I wanted something to eat. I shook my head and thanked her. It was time to go.

She accompanied me to the door, hugged me. "I'll call my father now," she said, and assured me they'd do what they could.

"Thank you," I said again.

She hugged me, this time for longer.

"Come back soon." Again, she sounded as if she meant it.

"I will," I said, almost believing it myself.

———

This morning I awoke and listened to the gentle traffic outside, the horns of the ships gliding past. Then I got up, took my coat, and walked outside. The snow on the pavement was powdery, shimmering in the sun like shredded glass. It's Sunday, and people were out in the streets, taking their families for a walk. I looked at all of them. It's an impulse I can't seem to shake, to look at everyone I pass, hoping to recognize a face in the crowd, yearning for the familiar.

I went toward the water—past the brownstones, their solid broad stairs leading up to the angels and stars and Santa Clauses in the windows; past the decorations, the abundance.

They buried the miners this week. They didn't even say anything about it on TV—Jarek told me. He'd heard about it from home. It seems hundreds of security forces were there to prevent riots—a funeral procession lined by men in helmets, in honor of those who were killed by men in helmets. I felt more sadness than anger. Maybe because the year is drawing to an end. There is only so much hatred you can produce, only so much resentment you can hold inside of you.

Yesterday I tried calling Granny again and the unthinkable

happened: the signal went through. Someone picked up the receiver.

"Hello?" I couldn't believe my luck, as if I'd thrown a rope across the ocean and she'd caught it. "How are you?" I asked, again and again, clutching the receiver until my palms turned oily.

Her voice was the same as ever. She was fine, she insisted, a little too much. She had enough to eat. She stayed in, mostly. She tried not to read the news or listen to what the neighbors said. Of course I knew that the line was tapped, that somewhere, in some sad, cramped radio room, someone was listening to us and that Granny was trying to say the right things.

"And you, Ludzio?"

"I'm all right," I said quickly. And then I told her that I was thinking of coming home. That—

"Don't," she said, interrupting me, her voice becoming urgent. "There is nothing here. Your suffering won't help us."

"Granny—" I tried, to stop her from incriminating herself, but she interrupted me again.

"Stay where you are," she said. "At least it gives me hope. And now hang up, my love," she added. "This call must be costing you millions."

I put down the receiver and buried my head in my hands.

Part of me still wanted to return. Even though I knew that, once there, they would never let me leave again. Even though I knew it was a folly, that I'd be a prisoner. But at least I'd be there. Inside.

I walked to the waterfront, to the broken-down piers. Across the foamy river the skyline of Manhattan was drawn against the sky, a hundred glistening Palaces of Culture assembled next

to one another, absorbing the December light. And looking at
that light, I thought of Christmas at home, the way we used to
spend it. I thought of Granny and Mother and me buying a carp
from the man in the street, picking the fattest one from those
swimming around in the metal basins standing on the pavement, pointing our gloved fingers at the same one. We would
take it home, let the bathwater run, and make it swim in the
tub. That was my favorite part. I would give it a name. I would
tell it that I'd take it to the Oder and release it. And I'd mean
it. But then Christmas Eve would come and I'd be hungry, and
Mother would be ready. She'd take it out of the bath like she'd
taken me out when I was small, careful not to drop it. Then
she would cut its head off. She would slice open the body and
scoop out its organs like the seeds of a grape, her hands as red
as the devil, blood trickling down her wrists and forearms all
the way to her elbows.

———

The day after I saw Hania, I didn't return to the Bureau, like
the man in the glasses had made me promise. I sat in my room,
stared at my watch, and imagined him at his desk, growing
agitated. Every minute after that, I expected a knock on the
door, militiamen taking me away or a representative from the
housing board handing me a notice of eviction. But none of
that came. Not the next day, and not the following one either.
The week drew to a close without anything unusual happening
at all. Except that it began to snow. Snow tumbled from pillow-
white clouds all over the city, dancing, giddy flakes, freshly
born, covering streets and houses and cars with a sparkling crust,
bringing everything to a halt for a moment.

One morning, soon afterward, *Pani* Kolecka knocked on my door and handed me a big brown envelope. Inside was a passport with a visa.

A couple of weeks later I saw Karolina for the last time. She was waiting for me outside in the snow, a large fur hat on her head, her breath visible in the cold. She smiled when she saw me.

"Why didn't you go inside?" I asked, nodding toward the door of the bar.

"I wanted to go in with you," she said, kissing me on the cheek, wrapping her arm around mine.

Inside, we were hit by the warm air, the looks of the patrons. Men, young and old, eyed us with barely concealed curiosity. Like last time, we sat near the bar and ordered two beers. They were playing Donna Summer's latest song, "Bad Girls." I tapped along with my fingers.

"Funny you would ask me to meet you here," said Karolina, smiling. "I thought you didn't like this place."

I laughed. "I changed my mind. That's allowed, right?"

"Encouraged," she said, enjoying herself.

The beers arrived, and we toasted. Karolina started telling me about the last few weeks, about her dates with Karol. They were in love.

"I am so glad for you," I said, and meant it. "So glad."

We ordered another round, toasted again.

"What about you?" she asked. "What was it you wanted to tell me?"

I took a long sip and began to tell her about you and me and Hania. The uncensored truth, for the first time. She gasped throughout but didn't seem too surprised. Until I told her about the passport.

"So you're . . . ?" Her eyes began to shimmer.

"Yes. Next week."

"That's great," she said, her voice breaking with emotion. She looked at her beer. "And can't you . . . wait?"

"I think it's time for me," I said. "And now that you're the one in love, I'm not going to ask you to come with me."

She looked up. Tears freed themselves from her eyes, drawing black paths of mascara down her cheeks. She cried noiselessly, and I took her into my arms. When she was done, she caught a glimpse of herself in the mirror behind the bar and wiped the traces of mascara with the back of her hand. "Look at me," she said, breaking out into a smile. "I'm a mess."

"Yes, you are," I said. "And I will miss you. Maybe you'll come and join me one day?"

"Maybe," she said, smiling, wiping away the rest of her tears.

The day before my plane departed, I went to a bookshop to find an English language manual. Walking into the shop, I saw you—your arm around her waist, looking at the table of books by the entrance. You were wearing a new leather jacket, brown, with a beautiful fur collar. And there was a moustache above your upper lip. I froze. It was Hania who looked up and saw me and smiled, and I had no choice but to walk over and say hello, my body numb. The air was impenetrable between us. She kissed me on the cheek; you and I shook hands solemnly. I could feel her looking from you to me with a quiet sort of concentration. Then she excused herself, said she was going to pay for the books. And there we stood, the two of us. You watched her go, avoiding my gaze. Finally you put your index and middle fingers toward your lips.

"Wanna smoke?"

We stepped outside under the awning of the bookshop, looking out onto the street. It was cold and sunny. Frost covered the pavement like icing. You took a packet of Marlboros from your pocket and handed me one.

"Nice moustache," I said, nervous, when you lit my cigarette, and you saw my eyes flicker over your face, your fingers grazing mine as you cupped your hands to protect the flame from the wind. You ignored my comment, its platitude. Instead, you lit your cigarette without looking at me and blew the smoke through your nostrils like you couldn't wait to get it out of you. Then you turned your head in my direction. Your eyes measured me. I sensed that you wanted to say something, readied my body for whatever it was that you needed to come out. Then the shop door swung open and Hania appeared, with a bag filled with books. We stood for a moment, uncomfortable, mourning the missed opportunity. We searched for words, each one of us, trying to say something that meant anything. In the end, we just said goodbye. We said it casually, like we would see each other again soon or maybe like people who had never been much more than acquaintances. You two walked off, arm in arm, and I watched you, the burning cigarette still in my hand, the last thing you'd ever given me.

———

I come back home from my walk, take off my coat, and rub my hands. I sit down on the couch and stare at the TV without switching it on.

I remember how I left our country and how I thought my

nightmare of loneliness would return. The nightmare of fossilized time, where I walk through the desolate landscape of overgrown gravestones, not a soul around, condemned to a life among the dead. But it didn't. I came to a new country, a new city, and decided to leave my loneliness behind. America is good like that. Even if it isn't true, even if you can't ever completely shed your past, no one here will tell you that. It makes it easier. Easier to fool yourself. You, of all people, must know what that feels like.

And yet, it occurs to me now that we can never run with our lies indefinitely. Sooner or later we are forced to confront their darkness. We can choose the when, not the if. And the longer we wait, the more painful and uncertain it will be. Even our country is doing it now—facing its archive of lies, wading through the bog toward some new workable truth.

Six months after I arrived here, Karolina sent me a letter about the wedding. That Hania had been pregnant during the ceremony, how it had already been visible. And I cried, despite myself. All this time I'd meant to ask you whether you loved her. It was the one thing that I regretted not asking. I realize now that it never mattered. Because you were right when you said that people can't always give us what we want from them; that you can't ask them to love you the way you want. No one can be blamed for that. And the odds had been stacked against us from the start: we had no manual, no one to show us the way. Not one example of a happy couple made up of boys. How were we supposed to know what to do? Did we even believe that we deserved to get away with happiness?

I go to the bookshelf and take out *Giovanni's Room*, run my fingers over its worn cover. I think of all the eyes that have passed over these pages, all the hands that have felt its weight. And I remember the day my plane was leaving, when *Pani* Kolecka came into my room for the last time, an envelope in her hand, with *Giovanni's Room* inside. I clutched it to my chest like a treasure long lost and now found again. When I opened it with a beating heart, a piece of paper fluttered out, landing gently on the floor.

"I adored this book more than you knew," it read there in your stocky, right-leaning script. *"I wanted to keep it . . . but it's yours. Bring it back one day if you can. I'll be here. J."*

All this time, I realize, I've lived like my departure was temporary, your words preventing me from ever really leaving or arriving. Despite Karolina's letter, despite the marriage, I've held on to the idea of us, scanning faces for a scrap of something known, searching for the familiar in the alien. When really, the familiar had already turned alien, and home had ceased being home. Both have gone on living and changing without me.

I close the book and place it back on the shelf, reach for my coat again, leave the apartment, and walk out into the street. The wind sweeps into my face, and I brace against it, walking toward the grocery stores on Eagle Street. My belly rumbles. I am hungry, suddenly, as if I haven't eaten in weeks. I want borscht and *pierogi* and warm poppy-seed cake, and I feel this as a vast, cavernous emptiness inside me, a yearning for warmth. But it isn't painful at all. It feels like a promise.

ACKNOWLEDGMENTS

The making of *Swimming in the Dark* was a seven-year journey, and it would have been impossible without the generosity and love of the following people:

Tanja Stege, Elizabeth Stephan, and Dr. Louis Monaco, who believed in me long before I did; Season Butler and all the members of our London writing group, who encouraged and nurtured Ludwik's world from the very start; my friends Hanaa Hakiki, Lottie Davey, Ella Delany, Manon Moreau, and Leila Brahimi, who gave me invaluable advice on the first drafts; my amazing agent, Sam Hodder; and my wonderful editors, Alexa von Hirschberg and Jessica Williams.

Without my parents—their courage, their resourcefulness, as well as their passion for storytelling—I would have never had the tools to write this book. *Dziękuję wam z całego serca.*

Lastly, I want to thank my best friend and husband for his unrivaled patience, support, and sense of humor: Laurent, *je t'aime.*

Insights,
Interviews
& More . . .

About the Author

About the Book

Meet Tomasz Jedrowski

Kuba Dabrowski

TOMASZ JEDROWSKI is a graduate of
Cambridge University and the Université
de Paris. Born in Germany to Polish
parents, he has lived in several countries,
including Poland, and currently lives
outside Paris. This is his first novel. ∾

An Interview with Tomasz Jedrowski

A version of this interview first appeared on Jezebel.com by Rich Juzwiak, May 13, 2020.

You speak five languages [Polish, English, French, German, and Spanish] but write in English. Is there anything about English specifically that has inspired your preference?

I've never properly thought about it, myself. I feel like English is a tool that hasn't been imposed on me. It's not something that I happened to be born into. It's just something I enjoyed from the very start, and I don't feel like it's my parents speaking through me when I'm writing in English, because we never spoke in English. I don't think it's society speaking through me, because I didn't grow up in an English-speaking society. It's my literary language, because it's in English that I really started reading books properly. It's this part of my mind that feels really intimate and private, but not the same as intimacy between me and my family or intimacy between me and my husband. It's sort of self-intimacy. ▶

An Interview with Tomasz Jedrowski
(continued)

Could you talk about the genesis of the book? What prompted you to write about two men in love in 1980 Poland?

For me the genesis of the book is closely linked to me deciding to write at all, when I dared to come out to myself as someone who actually wants to write. I used to be a lawyer and I [went through] therapy, because I didn't know what I wanted to do with my life. I found a writing course, and they asked me to write anything. I had decided I was going to be a writer, but I didn't have an idea. It was more the idea of being a writer that I liked. When I had to write this thing for my writing class, I had this flash in my mind where I could see this guy, who's a student, fancying this other guy and this sense of not really being able to live that love and also the other guy not feeling exactly the same. It was that image I started with and then I developed it.

Had it been brewing, though? I mean, do you identify as gay?

Yeah, I mean, I would say so. I came out as gay many years ago, but the reason I waited for such a long time is that I felt like it was such a prescribed identity and I didn't feel like I wanted to fit into that box. And then I was like, "Okay, in the absence of anything more accurate,

I will go with that." But it's funny because there's the moment in the book when Ludwik goes to see [his friend] Hania and he sort of tells her, "I'm a homosexual." I thought it was a really important scene but then I didn't want this to be the major message. Really what I care about is trying to discover those gray zones and, really, the truth. I guess when you put a label on something—"I am this"—we have to look at, "Well, what is this? What do people define it as?" I've always been more comfortable with what I *do*, with verbs rather than nouns.

I think it's a very complicated taxonomy, but there's a long history of gay men throwing other gay men under the bus by identifying as straight. A single word could never represent an entire human experience, but sometimes the absence of that word amounts to sheer deception.

Yes. It's important that we have vocabulary and also that we develop vocabulary. It *is* really complex, and it's also very subjective. Some people do it out of fear, and other people do it to control others, as a means of suppression. I've met some people like that in my life and I find them fascinating. I think that's where Janusz comes from. ▸

An Interview with Tomasz Jedrowski
(continued)

Did any of the premise of the book come from you wondering what life must have been like in the country from which your parents hail, back in the days when it was much harder to be out?

I had this scene in my mind of someone in a lecture hall, but it wasn't me. It was a man who used to be friends with my father. He's the first man that I met that identified as gay—openly so. I remember meeting him when I was 8, I was with my parents. I was very nervous about meeting him. I could just tell that we had something in common. I never thought about this guy, but when I had to think of a story that mattered to me, I saw him. I just assumed that he was in love with my father—the guy I saw this character fancying was my father. I wouldn't say Janusz is my father. I worked a lot on changing these characters and making them their own people, but that was the starting point.

It was just this weird, deep self-identification with this person, or rather with the projection of that person. When I started writing *Swimming in the Dark*, I went to Warsaw. I felt like I had to be there. I was researching and writing, and I gave him a call. We met up and it was a bit disillusioning. I had an image of him in my mind and he wasn't that. He was quite shocking in many ways. I grew up and my parents would tell me what Poland was like, and to me, in Western Germany in the '90s, it was the most exotic thing on earth. It was a time when the end of history was proclaimed. It was the end of the Cold War. The message was: We're going to be wealthier from year to year. To hear about a society that was so radically different, where you didn't know where things would come from, where there was so much uncertainty, I found it just wild. The novel was an excuse for me to research it and know more about it.

I appreciated many things about your use of Giovanni's Room, *but especially that it immediately contextualizes your book in the larger history of gay literature. Was that a conscious choice?*

I didn't really aim for this book to be part of all that. It didn't really occur to me that it could be. It wasn't conscious but I guess the reason why I used [*Giovanni's Room*] is because I wanted to pay homage to it. That's all it was. It was really a way to celebrate it. I felt so deeply grateful to the book, and I hadn't really been able to express it in any other way. Sure, I would speak to people here and there but I felt like no one really understood it. [That] book made me feel part of something, and that's what I wanted Ludwik to feel as well. It really comes as a revelation. It's not about *Swimming in the Dark* being part of all that, it was really about *Giovanni's Room* being ▶

An Interview with Tomasz Jedrowski
(continued)

an important voice that people needed
to hear, some people desperately.
Something that you thought was so
personal and so inside you that no one
could have possibly felt the same before,
but then when you read something
and you realize others had felt it, that's
when you become part of this, for lack
of a better word, a sort of brotherhood.
A tradition. A tradition of people
throughout history having thought
in similar ways. That's incredible.

I think of **Giovanni's Room** *as largely
a tragedy. So much of it is coated in
sadness, even the love—like when
David talks about Giovanni's love
awakening a beast, explaining,
"With this fearful intimation there
opened in me a hatred for Giovanni
which was as powerful as my love
and which was nourished by the same
roots." It's almost like a double helix of
emotions. Baldwin was so wise, a true
master of humanity, but your book isn't
nearly as melancholy.*

I recently opened *Giovanni's Room* and
I was struck by just how sad it was. I'd
sort of forgotten. I think the reason why
it spoke to me when I first read it, in
2008 in New York, is I think I *was* that
sad. When I started writing *Swimming
in the Dark*, I had a lot of sadness in me,
and I think it was a way of digesting it.
The first couple of years [writing it],

8

I didn't know where the book was going. I didn't know what I was trying to do with it. I knew it was an unhappy love story. I'd written scenes where Ludwik was desperately in love with Janusz and threw himself out of a window and then he sat in a hospital. I had to get all of that out. I was reading it, thinking, "This is so over the top. This is not good literature. There's nothing to learn from this." It was kind of what I was going through in life as well. I didn't really know where I was going. I didn't really have a formula for how to live and what I believed in. And then I did this meditation course, a 10-day silent retreat, and I came out of that course and felt like my brain had been rewired. I accepted in my life for the first time that I wanted to be happy, that I wanted to feel joy. I think it was because of all of the years of suppressing who I was. When I started writing again, I could finally see that I could give Ludwik hope, because I had actually found it.

Did you have any philosophy regarding writing about sex?

I didn't have a strategy. I wanted something that would feel real. For me, sensuality is really, really important. It's funny because when they first have sex and Ludwik enumerates Janusz's body parts and at the end, he says, "Cock," in the Polish translation they ▶

An Interview with Tomasz Jedrowski
(continued)

censored that to "you know what." To be
honest, I had the idea of wanting it to be
tasteful, whatever that means. I didn't
feel the need to shock, I didn't want
anything too graphic, but I definitely
wanted them to enjoy the sex. I wanted
that sense of you losing your head a little
bit, like when sex makes you lose your
head and transforms time and makes
everything else unimportant. That's
what it can be like, especially when
you're discovering it with someone
you care about.

Do you feel pressure for your next book?

Some, but I think writing is really the
opposite of feeling all of those things.
Writing is connecting with other voices
and connecting with the subconscious
and drowning out the external world.
When I'm actually writing, I don't feel
pressure, but sometimes I have that
little voice saying, "Oh, but what will
reviewers say about that?" which I never
had before. But it's an amazing luxury to
have that. This is going to sound weird,
but I look forward to disappointing
people. What I'm writing now is so
different from *Swimming in the Dark*, so
I know already that there are going to be
readers that are going to be disappointed.
That's their right. And again, that's a
luxury, presuming that people will even
be interested in the next book. ᴄᴧ

Behind the Book

Whenever I consider the origins of *Swimming in the Dark*, I first think of my childhood.

Though I was born and raised in Germany, we visited Poland often once the Wall came down. We'd go to see my grandmother in Wroclaw or an aunt in Warsaw, or my parents would send my sister and me to Catholic summer camps. I spoke the language, but the country made me feel like a foreigner. I dreaded its grayness, its rusty playgrounds, the sound our car made over the cracked roads. Even the people were rougher. It was there, at barely six years old, that I was first called "faggot," by some boys at a camp. I didn't know the meaning of the word, but I guessed that it was something shameful that applied to me.

Back in Bremen, I would shudder at the thought that I could have been born in Poland had my parents not fled the country before my birth. As young graduates with no contacts in the Communist Party, they'd tried to make do with the empty shops, the endless queues, the hopeless, underpaid jobs. Until they managed to obtain passports and slip out of the country. Until their despair outgrew their fear of the unknown, promised West, a place they'd only ever seen on the silver screen.

When I first started writing *Swimming in the Dark*, this turning point in my parents' lives, and therefore my own, ▶

11

felt particularly poignant. It struck me how arbitrary our birthplaces can be, how arbitrary privilege really is. I began to imagine what life would have been like had I been born just a little earlier, and a little more east. How could I have lived and loved in dignity in Communist Poland? What sacrifices would I have had to make? And would I have, invariably, yearned for the freedoms of the capitalist world?

As the story began to take shape, I increasingly felt the pull of home, for the world in which the novel was set and where its budding characters lived; I flew to Warsaw. It was the first time I'd been back in a long time, and the first by myself. I walked the streets of the former Jewish ghetto, built over with concrete housing blocks, rode the tram through the working-class *Praga* district, where, like stars, bullet holes from WWII still adorned the façades, and explored the elegant neighbourhoods south of the center. Who had lived in these different houses, I wondered, when everyone was supposed to have been equal under the former system? And what had they done to get there?

Throughout this process of writing, research, and travel, *Giovanni's Room* accompanied me. James Baldwin's second novel was the first book about same-sex love that I ever read. I discovered it in my early twenties and never before had I felt so wholly understood. Never before had I known that a book could possess such healing power. I wanted Ludwik, the young narrator of *Swimming in the Dark*, to have a similarly meaningful experience with Baldwin's novel: to help him recognize his shame as something others had lived through before, to allow him to overcome it in the quest of becoming himself.

In the Poland of today, such need for comfort and reassurance continues to be a necessity. Out of fear, countless LGBTQ+ people still hide their true identities from their families, friends, and colleagues. As that peculiar midpoint between Berlin and Moscow, Polish society finds itself torn between tolerance and "traditional" values. But this conflict also mirrors a global phenomenon, one that spares next to no country. Now, perhaps more than ever, we need to draw strength and solace from the stories of others, and to share our own. ༄

Questions for Discussion

1. How did the use of second-person narration affect your reading experience?

2. Think about the power literature holds for the characters in this novel. Why are books so often targets of restriction and censorship?

3. How does Jedrowski contrast the Polish cities and the countryside? How does setting influence the characters' actions and attitudes?

4. The version of reality that Ludwik learns about in school stands in sharp contrast to the whispered truths he garners from his family and books. Have you ever felt that you were receiving two sides of a story? How do you decide which is real?

5. Ludwik and Janusz's connection is utterly unthinkable in their society—not simply condemned, but not even acknowledged as possible. How does this affect their ability to identify their own feelings and form a connection?

6. Think about the imagery of water in *Swimming in the Dark*. What does water represent, and how does the metaphor transform throughout the novel?

7. Despite Ludwik and Janusz's passionate love for each other, they find themselves on the opposite sides of an ideological divide. Have you ever experienced such a division with someone you care about? When are these differences worth overcoming, or not?

8. Why did some Polish citizens accept and play into a corrupt government? Who was gaining from this system?

9. What kinds of freedoms are the characters in *Swimming in the Dark* fighting for? Does freedom always come at a cost?

10. How does *Swimming in the Dark* demonstrate the failures of communism in practice? What does true equality look like, and is it possible for us to achieve it?

11. Think about Ludwik's and Janusz's coming of age in this novel. How do their attitudes, perceptions, and desires change as they grow up? Are these changes for better or worse?

12. Ludwik admits, ". . . people can't always give us what we want from them . . . you can't ask them to love you the way you want." How do you interpret this statement? Do you think ▶

Questions for Discussion *(continued)*

Ludwick or Janusz is at fault for what happened to their relationship?

13. What do you make of Ludwik's and Janusz's ultimate decisions about how they will live their lives? Do you think either made the wrong choice, or do you sympathize with both? How might things have changed if either had made a different decision?

14. Think about these lines: "We can never run with our lies indefinitely. Sooner or later we are forced to confront their darkness. We can choose the when, not the if. And the longer we wait, the more painful and uncertain it will be." How does this theme express itself throughout the novel, for the characters and the country? ∾